Secret Schemes and Daring Dreams

Rosie Rushton lives in Northampton. She is a governor of the local Church of England secondary school, a licensed lay minister and passionate about all issues relating to young people. Her hobbies include learning Swahili, travelling, going to the theatre, reading, walking, being juvenile with her grandchildren and playing hopscotch when no one is looking. Her ambitions are to write the novel that has been pounding in her brain for years but never quite made it to the keyboard, to visit China, learn to sing in tune, and do anything else God has in mind for her, with a broad grin and a spring in her step. Her many books for Piccadilly Press include *Friends, Enemies and Other Tiny Problems; Secrets of Love* and several series including *The Leehampton Quartet* and *What a Week*.

Secret Schemes and Daring Dreams

ROSIE RUSHTON

Piccadilly Press • London

First published in Great Britain in 2008
by Piccadilly Press Ltd,
5 Castle Road, London NW1 8PR
www.piccadillypress.co.uk

A catalogue record for this book is available from the
British Library

ISBN: 978 1 85340 942 4 (paperback)

1 3 5 7 9 10 8 6 4 2

Printed and bound in Great Britain by CPI Bookmarque, Croydon
Cover illustration by Susan Hellard
Cover design by Simon Davis
Text design by Carolyn Griffiths, Cambridge
Set in Goudy and Caslon

Mixed Sources
Product group from well-managed
forests and other controlled sources
www.fsc.org Cert no. TT-COC-002227
© 1996 Forest Stewardship Council
FSC

For Celia Rees, whose writing is inspirational and whose support for this book was unfailing; and for all those members of the Scattered Authors Society whose encouragement kept me going when none of the characters would behave themselves. Thank you. And to Vince Cross, for initiating a totally uncool author into the mysteries of the gig circuit!

❧ CHAPTER 1 ❧

Secret scheme:
Maximum street-cred for minimum effort

EMMA WOODHOUSE HAD, FOR SEVENTEEN YEARS AND TEN months, had pretty much everything in life her own way (if you overlook the unfortunate death of her mother before she was out of nappies, and that large spot on her right cheek on the night of the South Downs Ball), and she saw no reason at all why the situation should ever change. She was of the opinion that, if you wanted something enough, you simply applied all your energies to getting it. She had no time for wimps, and even less for people who started sentences with 'I can't'. But she was above all a caring and considerate sort of girl, who was well aware of her own good fortune, stunning looks and talent for getting the best out of other people. Which was why, when she met someone with untapped potential, she put all her own interests to one side and set out to change their lives for them. Whether they liked it or not.

Her most recent triumph had been the sorting out of

her best friend's love life. Lucy Taylor was the kind of girl who made choosing the wrong guy into an art form. She either got herself mixed up with total losers because she felt sorry for them and couldn't say no when they asked her out; or else she fell dramatically in love with guys who were way out of her league, and hardly noticed her existence, with the result that she cried for days and went round with puffy eyes and snot on the end of her nose.

So, when Emma discovered that India Hood from the tennis club had dumped the super-fit Adam Weston in favour of some geek she had met on a field trip to the Orkneys, she had seized the moment and organised a double date (even enduring the company of the slimy Simon Wittering for a whole evening for the sake of her friend's future happiness, and that was sacrifice in anyone's book). As she had expected, her ploy had worked. Adam was perfect for Lucy – he had a great bum and a cute smile; and while Emma would have found his intellect seriously unchallenging, she had reckoned – correctly, of course – that he was well within Lucy's comfort zone. What's more, he was doing a sports degree at Bournemouth, which meant that every weekend he bombed up the A27 in his lime-green Beetle to see her in Brighton. This was something of a relief all round, since by Thursday mornings, Lucy was pining big time and playing 'he loves me, he loves me not' with any unfortunate flower that happened to be within her grasp.

They had been an item now for five whole months, which broke any record Lucy had ever achieved. She went around with a permanent grin on her face, even after a weekend of watching basketball, or cricket or whatever sport was Adam's module for the month; she kept O_2 in business with her constant text messaging, and repeatedly told Emma that she had never been so happy and owed it all to her.

Her only complaint was that she was strapped for cash.

'Adam pays for almost everything,' she had confided to Emma after she had been with Adam for six weeks, 'but it's not like he's loaded and, somehow, it doesn't feel quite right.'

'Absolutely not!' Emma had agreed. 'You need to show him that you are an independent, self-supporting woman of the twenty-first century.'

'I guess you're right,' Lucy had said reluctantly.

'Of course I am.' Emma had refrained from letting on that she was quoting, almost verbatim, her own father's words. Despite being extremely wealthy and perfectly capable of funding Emma, he had refused to contribute to her gap year unless she earned at least some of the money. There had been a lot of talk about the world not owing her a living and the country going to ruin because of a lack of committed work ethic. Emma had nodded obediently and told him that she'd get a job just as soon as A-levels were over. She had then decided, quite firmly, that burger bars, department stores and seaside cafés were not on her agenda; but that, if she could find a job with good networking opportunities and hours flexible enough to accommodate all the social events that were already stacking up in her diary, she would give it her best shot. And then she put the whole thing out of her mind.

Over the weeks since exams had finished her father had made a few ridiculous suggestions about jobs, all of which she had rejected out of hand. Who in their right mind would work eight hours a day dressed as a Regency housemaid and handing out guidebooks at the Royal Pavilion? And as for packing organic veggie boxes for the local farm shop, forget it: as she explained to her father, you don't pay zillions for a French manicure and then deal with unwashed carrots. It was when he began talking about cleaning up graffiti on run-down housing estates and mending hedges in Northumberland that she realised she had to do something to get him off her back.

So she was somewhat relieved when the perfect solution presented itself. Not only the perfect, and basically undemanding, part-time job for her; but more importantly, a little money-spinner for Lucy, who was in the throes of one of her 'I'm so useless, no one would employ me' premenstrual cycles. OK, so when Emma told her about the plan, she did seem a little distracted and less enthusiastic than she'd hoped, but she put that down to the fact that Lucy was hyperventilating over her upcoming driving test and, once that was over, she'd be speechless with gratitude.

So the last thing that Emma expected at nine o'clock on the leavers' evening of her final term at Deepdale Hall, the exclusive co-ed day school on the outskirts of Brighton, was to have all her carefully laid plans thrown into disarray.

The evening had started so well: the in-crowd had met up on the roof garden of the Freaked Out Frog (which as anyone with style and savvy will know is just about the coolest place in Brighton to hang out on a hot summer evening) and Emma had instantly been the centre of attention. This had a lot to do with the fact that she had just dished out a batch of tickets for Shellshocked's Gig on the Beach later in July, courtesy of her father. Her dad was the Seventies rock star, now turned eco-warrior, Tarquin Tee (he had never thought Woodhouse was a suitable name for him – 'sounds too much like woodlouse' he used to say). Although Tarquin no longer made the centre pages of *MusicMaker* magazine, or headlined at gigs, he was very much in the public eye, fronting TV's *Going Green* programme, appearing in ads for energy-saving light bulbs and hybrid cars, and regularly lambasting MPs about their carbon footprints. In Emma's set, having a parent with a name suitable for dropping into conversations was a decided asset, and Tarquin still had enough contacts to be able to get tickets for all the best gigs. Emma felt able to forgive some of his more way-out idiosyncrasies in return for being flavour of the month with the entire Sixth Form.

'I can't go,' Lucy had said as Emma tossed a ticket in her direction. 'I'll be working.'

'Working?' Serena Middleton-Hyde fiddled ostentatiously with the clasp on her Gucci bag and stared at Lucy in amazement. 'Whatever for?'

'Money,' Lucy retorted. 'I need to save up for – well, things.'

'Oh don't worry, I'll get you the time off,' Emma assured her hastily. 'I've got loads of influence with the Knightleys.'

'The Knightleys?' Chelsea Finch had exclaimed, turning to Lucy. 'You're going to be working at their hotel? Donwell Abbey?'

'It's not a hotel,' Emma informed her sharply. 'It's a Country House Experience. And yes, Lucy and I have got jobs to die for – right, Lucy?'

'Well, yes, but actually . . .'

'What? You as well?' Serena interjected, draping an arm seductively around Angus MacKenzie. 'How can you bear to spend the summer slogging your guts out for a pittance when you could be partying on the beach at Rock like us?'

Emma, who had absolutely no intention of slogging for five minutes let alone a whole season, pushed her shades on to the top of her head and gave Serena one of her most withering looks. 'Why would we waste the summer getting trashed with a load of airheads when we could be mixing with celebs?'

As she had hoped, her words had an immediate effect.

'Celebs? Like who?' Serena demanded suspiciously.

'All sorts,' Emma declared. 'Donwell attracts the A-list' (it wasn't a complete lie – a *Blue Peter* presenter had stayed there only a month ago) 'and besides, Today TV are going to be filming an episode of *Going Green* in the village. Dad reckons Lucy and I might get filmed too.'

'I get split shifts at Happy Hamburger – you get a manor house, champagne lifestyle and instant fame!' Tabitha Baxter burst out.

'That's because some of us won't settle for second best,' Emma commented calmly. 'Right, Lucy?'

'What? Oh. Yeah, right.' Lucy seemed nervy and out

of sorts and suddenly Emma realised why. Clearly the thought of the new job was suddenly getting to her – she had always been a bit on the shy side, and a Grade One worrier. Donwell Abbey was the ancestral home of the Knightleys, who were close friends of Emma's dad; the house stood halfway up a hillside above the village of Ditchdean, four miles from Brighton, its mullioned windows catching glimpses of the English Channel in one direction and the South Downs in another. Emma's home, Hartfield, stood in its extensive grounds and had once been the Dower House of the estate. Emma had played with the Knightley boys, George and John, since she was in nursery and, as a result, treated the whole place as if it were her own.

Thirteen generations of Knightleys had lived at Donwell, but sadly the first ten had spent money like water, and Guy and Candida Knightley, the eleventh generation, had died within a few months of one another, which thrilled the men at the Inland Revenue who were in charge of death duties, but did nothing to ease the way for their descendants. Emma had still been a little kid, riding her pony in the Knightleys' paddock, when the deer park was turned into a golf course, and the lake on which she and George acted out *Swallows and Amazons* when it was stocked with trout and leased out to local anglers in the hope of raising money. The tack room became a tearoom and the orangery was turned into a small health club, much to the delight of the middle classes of the surrounding villages and the local suppliers of Lycra bodywear. The extensive gardens were open to the public every weekend and children were kept occupied on the Woodland Walk and Nature Trail complete with Tarzan-style rope swings and hollow logs for hide-and-seek. Despite all this, the upkeep of thirty rooms and the remaining twenty acres was a huge burden and so, when George's father, Max Knightley, overheard a visitor to one of his Open Gardens days the previous season remark that it 'wouldn't half be good to live like the gentry for a bit', he had the brainwave of turning his home into a place where social climbers could live out their fantasies while paying handsomely for the privilege. It was, he declared, to be very tasteful: just a dozen or so guests for a long weekend and the atmosphere of a nineteenth-century house party. Emma thought it was hilarious; but clearly Lucy was totally intimidated by the whole thing.

'Look, you guys,' Emma announced as Lucy's nail-biting frenzy increased, 'I need to check some stuff out with Lucy – catch you later, OK?'

She seized Lucy by the arm, picked up her drink and dragged her to the one available bench overlooking the crowded street below. It was the warmest evening of the summer so far, and the fountains in the square were a magnet for slightly inebriated holidaymakers and snogging couples. This was the Brighton Emma loved: its seafront tackiness, the fading splendour of its Regency architecture and the constant swooping and squawking of the seagulls as they hunted for discarded ice-cream cones and decaying bits of doughnut.

'Listen, there's something I've got to tell you.' Lucy began speaking before Emma had the chance to launch into her impromptu pep talk. 'And I know you won't like it . . .' She looked as agitated as she had on the day she had confessed to losing Emma's favourite shirt.

'It's OK, I know what you're going to say,' Emma assured her.

'You do?'

'I guess it's about the job.'

'Well, yes, it is actually. You see, the thing is . . .'

'Look, you don't have to worry!' Emma butted in, sipping her Summer Cooler. 'It's not even like you've got to live in at Donwell – you're staying at my place, and you've done that enough times!'

'Yes, but listen . . .'

'Honestly, it's going to be so cool. You only have to waitress for breakfast and dinner . . .'

'Will you just shut up a minute!' Lucy burst out, her freckled face flushing. 'I'm not taking the job.'

'Not taking it?' Emma stared at her open-mouthed. 'What are you on about? Of course you're taking it – you can't let nerves get in the way of an opportunity like this.'

'It's got nothing to do with nerves. I applied for another job a couple of weeks ago, and this morning I heard that I'd got it,' Lucy admitted, sipping her drink and avoiding eye contact with Emma.

'Oh, is that all?' Emma shrugged. 'No probs – you can back out of it. We'll think up a really good excuse and, if you want me to write the letter, that's fine. I'm good with words.'

'I don't want to back out of it,' Lucy protested. 'I'm over the moon about it. See, it's with Adam. At the Frontier Adventure Centre. He's got a job as sports instructor and I'm going to be a lifeguard and swimming coach.'

'Lucy, what are you on?' Emma demanded. 'What's that going to look like on your CV?'

'I don't care about my CV.'

'Well you should – you need to be more ambitious,' Emma retorted. 'Besides, you can't back out now. Not with George's dad at death's door and him coping single-handed to keep the place afloat.'

When push came to shove, Emma regarded exaggeration as a perfectly legitimate tool to getting her own way.

'Death's door?' For an instant, Lucy looked guilt-ridden.

'Well, pretty much. And you know what that family mean to me,' Emma added, with what she hoped was a pitiful sigh. It wasn't a lie: all the time Emma and her sister, Bea – who was four years older than her – had been growing up, Sara and Max Knightley had been like second parents to them, having them to stay regularly, helping with fancy dress costumes, period pains and all the other things that motherless girls worry about, and even, as they got older, taking them on holiday with them to their house in Provence. George's older brother, John, was totally besotted with Bea (and had been for years, even before they went off to do voluntary work together in somewhere unpronounceable in South East Asia), with the result that George had somehow adopted the big brother role in Emma's life.

'And besides, I've already told George you'll be there,' Emma finished.

'Well, you'll just have to un-tell him,' Lucy said emphatically, scooping her ash-blond hair into a ponytail. 'I'm going to be with Adam and that's that.'

'Oh, so now he's on the scene I don't count, right?' Emma snapped, unexpected tears pricking behind her eyes.

'It's all about you now, is it?' Lucy replied, a flush spreading across her freckled face. 'Anyway, who was it that got Adam and me together in the first place? You!'

'I know but . . .'

' "Hey Lucy, he's so right for you! Go for it." ' That's what you said. Well, that's what I'm doing.'

Lucy took another swig of her drink.

'But that doesn't mean you have to take some crummy job,' Emma pleaded.

'It's not crummy. I want to work with kids, and this is a great opportunity. Anyway, being with Adam is what counts. I thought you'd be pleased for me. You said that you wanted me to be with the right guy and now I am.'

It occurred to Emma that Lucy would never have been so assertive in the old days. 'I'm sorry,' she said. 'I suppose I'm being selfish.'

'Look, I'll get us another drink!' Before Emma could speak, Lucy had jumped up and was heading towards the bar, clearly anxious to take advantage of Emma's apology to cool things a bit.

Emma sighed. She felt gutted; if there was one thing to which she was not accustomed, it was having her schemes scuppered before they had even got off the ground. For the past ten years, it had always been Emma who had taken the lead and set the rules and Lucy who had been willing to fit in with whatever scheme or dream she had cooked up. They hung out together at weekends; they decided which boys were fit and which definitely weren't; and every summer Lucy spent at least a month at Emma's house while Mrs Taylor, a high-flying art historian, hurtled round the world talking about Botticelli and Bruegel. And now here was Lucy leaning on the bar and joking with a couple of guys from the art college. She'd never have had the nerve to do that in the past, but, ever since she'd got it together with Adam back at Easter, she had been a different girl. She dressed more sassily and was positively brimming with newfound confidence.

What's more, she was making her own decisions and that was something that Emma found very inconvenient.

'Hey, Emma, what do you say you and I go down to Mango Monkey's right now and get hammered?'

Emma's musings were interrupted by Simon Wittering, who was digging her in the ribs, splashing her ankles with lager and leering at her.

'Get a life!' When dealing with idiots, Emma believed in cutting to the chase.

'That's just what I intend to do.' Simon laughed. 'Just think – a whole summer of boozing and bonk—'

'You,' declared Emma, standing up and giving him a withering look, 'are so sad it's unreal. But then again, the absence of that other "b" must be a real problem for you.'

'Er – what?'

'Brain, Simon, brain. Not having one must be such a handicap.'

'Hell, Emma, you can be so up yourself at times,' Simon snapped, taking another swig of lager. 'I don't know why I bother wasting my time talking to you.'

'Me neither,' Emma replied sweetly. 'So may I suggest you give us both a break and simply shut up?'

Simon was hardly out of earshot before Lucy was at Emma's elbow. 'So come on, what did he say? Did he ask you out again? Did you say yes?'

'Oh puh-leese!' Emma exclaimed, sticking two fingers into her mouth and making gagging noises. 'Funnily enough, I prefer *not* to go out with adolescent schoolboys. If you ask me the only things testosterone seems to hand out are spots and sweaty armpits.'

Lucy burst out laughing. 'Clearly this is your PMT week, right?'

'Could be,' Emma admitted, trying to laugh it off despite the knot in the pit of her stomach. It wasn't hormones that were making her edgy – it was the sudden realisation that everything was changing and there was nothing she could do about it. At school she had been the trendsetter since Year Seven, and everyone aspired to be in her set. But she had enough common sense to realise that it wasn't always going to be like that. Once she was at uni, she wouldn't be the centre of anyone's universe. And after the life she had led, that would take some getting used to.

She had only been a baby when her mother died, and too small to be affected by the scandal surrounding her death (*Rock star's wife found dead in swimming pool during drug-fuelled rave at Florida mansion*), but the impact on her father had been cataclysmic. Convinced that it was all his fault – an opinion encouraged by the press of the day, who painted him as irresponsible and reckless, he vowed to change everything about his life and start again. Within a year he had sold his houses in America and London, ditched the fast cars, abandoned the club scene and moved himself and his adored daughters to Sussex. He vowed there and then to devote himself to making amends for his previous hedonistic lifestyle by doing good works and nurturing the planet.

Sixteen years on, Tarquin was still totally committed to all things green, to the point, Emma sometimes thought, of neurosis. When he held dinner parties at Hartfield, he served only locally grown organic food, and English wine that was made from grapes that had been consulted as to their feelings during planting. He was so fussy about meat that he refused to eat it unless he knew not only the farm that it came from but the name and family history of the particular cow or sheep he was consuming. His house was fitted with solar panels in the roof, painted with non-toxic paints and insulated with recycled newspaper and, in an attempt to be carbon neutral, he had bought a hybrid car, a lawnmower that ran on some disgusting concoction that smelled like rotting fish and was now talking about installing composting toilets. At this, Emma had firmly drawn the line and threatened to leave home.

'You're not really miffed with me, are you?' Lucy nudged her out of her daydream and shoved a J_2O in front of her. 'I can't bear us to fall out.'

'No – I guess I did push you into it a bit,' Emma replied with a sigh.

'And the rest,' Lucy added with a hint of a smile.

'It was for your own good and besides, I'll – well, I'll miss you . . .'

'Don't be silly, I'll only be in the next village!' Lucy insisted. 'And I'll have loads of free time – we can hang

out like we always do. You can come over to my chalet—'
Lucy broke off as her mobile blared out her latest
ringtone.

Emma shuddered inwardly. How could Lucy even
think of spending the summer in some grotty camp
chalet and bobbing about in tepid water with a crowd of
snotty kids when she could be at Donwell? It didn't
make sense.

'It's Adam,' Lucy said, waving her mobile in Emma's
face. 'He's over at Mango's. Are you coming?'

'I guess.' Emma drained her drink and picked up her
bag. 'Oh, and while you've got the phone, you'd better
call George and let him know you're dropping him in it.'

She knew the remark was a bit below the belt but the
way she was feeling, she was beyond caring.

'You tell him,' Lucy replied calmly. 'After all, you set it
up and besides, like you said, you know him better.'

This calls for crisis management, thought Emma, as
they dodged the traffic in the Old Steyne and headed for
the club. She knew that, if she wasn't very careful, her
father would insist that she took on Lucy's job, and she'd
always been so careful to steer clear of anything that
involved washing up or bed-making.

Only half listening to Lucy's chatter about Adam's
gorgeous body, Emma cast her mind back to the previous
Tuesday morning when George, who was twenty-two
and usually very laid back, had turned up at Hartfield in
a state of high agitation.

'You won't believe what's happened,' he had gabbled,
sinking down on to one of the ancient kitchen chairs
that her father had rescued from Remainders Recycled,

and running his hand distractedly through his unruly dark-brown hair. 'Mum's just phoned. You know they're in Cape Town for their silver wedding anniversary?'

'Sadly, yes.' Tarquin had sighed. 'All those air miles. I did suggest the Shetland Isles but they weren't keen. I just hope they're off-setting . . .'

'So what's the matter?' Emma had cut in, seeing the anxiety in George's eyes.

'Mum got mugged . . .'

'No!' Tarquin had gasped.

'And Dad, idiot that he is, went to chase after the thugs that did it. They hit him over the head and stuck a knife in his chest.'

George had swallowed hard and gazed out of the window.

'Oh my God, is he . . .?' Emma had cried.

'He's concussed and got stitches and stuff, but the doctors say he should be OK. The thing is their passports were in Mum's bag and now the authorities won't let them go till they've got new ones.'

He had paused and bit into a slice of carrot cake that Emma had thoughtfully placed in front of him. ('No additives, GM free,' Tarquin had assured him as if George cared).

'It could take another week,' he had continued. 'At least. And they've got to wait till Dad is let out of hospital.'

'Well, not to worry,' Tarquin had begun. 'The main thing is that your father's in one piece.'

'Not to worry!' George had exploded, spitting cake crumbs over a wide area. 'You don't get it. Honestly, I knew Mum and Dad – well, they weren't exactly operating Donwell on a commercially viable basis, but it's chaos! The builders haven't finished decorating the new bedrooms over the stables . . .'

'I told your father they were cowboys,' Tarquin had muttered, 'but would he listen?'

'. . . And the Health and Safety people want handrails and loads of stupid signs saying, *Caution – Water* outside by the pool before we can open it again. So I phone Mum, and what does she say? Tells me to keep things afloat until they get back. Like I'm supposed to know what to do!'

'Well, you are doing an MBA,' Tarquin had pointed out calmly. 'And it will be good practice for you – most upcoming entrepreneurs would give their eye-teeth for hands-on experience like this!'

'That's the whole point,' George had insisted impatiently. 'Without Mum and Dad here, we don't have enough hands. You remember we lost our chef to Seafood 'n' Swallow last month? Well, yesterday the two girls who do waitressing for us at weekends announced that they are going too. Said the pay was better.'

'Tricky – but at least you've got Mrs P,' Tarquin had reasoned. Mrs Palmer, a huge woman with a heart of gold and very firm ideas about traditional cooking, had been with the family as a cook and housekeeper for as long as anyone could remember and had been seriously put out when the new chef was installed in her kitchen; she called him 'a foreigner fiddler with food'.

'Well, yes, obviously,' George had replied, 'but treacle pudding and fruit scones are hardly cutting-edge cuisine for the new millennium, are they? The agency sent a substitute chef for the upmarket stuff, but that still leaves us without a waitress or anyone to do the bar or help out in the kitchen when Mrs P's off.'

'So can't the agency find waitresses?' Tarquin had asked.

'Most of them are Eastern Europeans and Dad's adamant that we keep the thing traditionally English,' George answered. 'God knows what he'll say about this Luigi guy.' He sighed. 'Besides, they charge a bomb in commission and you can't have them on a casual basis – they all want contracts and everything. Which would be fine if my sainted parents had managed the place properly. But no – their advertising is crap . . .'

'George!'

'Sorry, but it is, and so what happens? We get a weekend with a full house then two weekends with only a smattering. He paused before continuing. 'I've been looking at the figures and between you and me, this season is crucial for us. Dad seriously overspent on the spa last year – he really is Mismanagement Incorporated. The bank is moaning and now Dad's losing interest and saying that, if we don't start making decent profits, he's going to sell up. Shepherd Hotels are already interested in turning the whole place into a conference centre.'

'Some profit-making, commercial cowboys as my next-door neighbours? No way!' Tarquin had looked shocked. 'Well, we'll just have to make certain this summer is a roaring success, won't we?'

'Sure,' George had replied sarcastically. 'For success

you need to set the right tone and, whatever the parents don't do right, they are pretty good hosts. Mum does all the meet and greet and charming the socks off people and running around arranging days out, and Dad does the bar and chats up the brides-to-be and that is *so* not my scene . . .'

At which point, Emma had assured him that he need worry no more. She pointed out that someone like her, who had been accepted to study psychology and human behavioural sciences at uni could only be an asset; and, of course, her interpersonal skills were second to none. (She knew this because her father told everyone whenever he got the chance.)

'And don't forget, I was a real hit last year when I did the serving wench thing at the medieval banquet,' she had reminded him.

'But this would be real work, Emma – not prancing around in a plunge neckline pouring glasses of mead,' George had retorted. 'What if you break a fingernail?'

'Better than you bursting a blood vessel every five seconds,' she had snapped back. 'Besides, I'm not offering to waitress. As if. Lucy can do that. She'll be thrilled.'

She smiled at George. 'I'll do all the meet and greet bit,' she had announced. 'Just till your parents are home again. Only not Tuesday mornings because that's massage and hair, and then next Saturday there's a gig on – oh, and Lucy's birthday is . . .'

'Real help you'll be then!' George had snapped. 'I'll just tell the guests that they mustn't need anything until they've checked your diary!'

'Forget it,' Emma had said. 'Either you want my skills or you don't, and frankly —'

'Skills? Airs and graces more like!' George had countered. 'You've always been the same —'

'Oh great – so who put sandpaper on your loo seat, then?' Emma had barked back.

'Will you two stop it right now!' Tarquin had ordered. 'Honestly, anyone would think you were still children arguing over who should go up the ladder to the tree house first!'

George had looked at Emma, and she had stared back. Then they had both burst out laughing. Admittedly, George's laughter had only lasted a millisecond, but it was long enough, to Emma's intense relief, for her father to step in and agree that it did make sense to employ Emma and Lucy (both such lovely girls) rather than pay exorbitant agency fees.

'And what's more, I'll help when I can,' Tarquin had said magnanimously. 'After all, you are my favourite godson and, besides, I've always wanted to do a feasibility study on solar lighting for the tennis court. Lovely people your parents, but when it comes to protecting the environment . . .'

'OK, Blob, you're on,' George had cut in hastily, and Emma had managed not to yell at him for using her childhood nickname. 'And you're sure Lucy will be up for it?'

'Trust me, she'll be over the moon,' Emma had assured him. 'She needs the money and being with me will be the icing on the cake!'

How on earth am I going to magic a replacement?

thought Emma now, as she and Lucy crossed Pool Valley to the lime-green and orange façade of Mango Monkey's. Because no way am I going to be up at seven every morning serving porridge to a load of pretentious old fogies.

Little did she know that, at that very moment, the answer to her prayers was sitting in a corner of the club, crying quietly into her strawberry and banana fizz.

⚡ CHAPTER 2 ⚡

Daring dream:
Rags to riches, courtesy of Emma W

MOST OF THE GANG WERE ALREADY SITTING AT THE BAR or strutting their stuff on the neon-lit dance floor by the time Emma and Lucy arrived. And within seconds, Lucy was draped all over Adam and indulging in some interesting lip aerobics. Emma, while being as open-minded as the next person, had no real desire to be an up-close spectator, and certainly was not going to succumb to the banal come-ons of Simon and his drooling mates. She glanced around the dimly-lit club in the hopes of spotting someone she knew with whom she could have an intelligent conversation.

'Isn't that Harriet?' she murmured, nudging Serena who was queuing with Tabitha at the bar. 'Over there in the corner?'

Serena peered across the room. 'What on earth is she doing here?' she muttered. 'Pretend you haven't see her – she's probably with the rest of the saddos from Mouldy Hill.'

Emma glared at her. When Mole Hill Secondary, the

worst sink school in town, had been the target of an arson attack, Deepdale Hall had offered to take Harriet and the few other sixth formers so that they could finish their A-level studies. As Mrs Goddard, the elegant and charismatic principal, explained to her privileged pupils, it behoved them all to share their good fortune with those to whom life had dealt a raw deal. (She failed to mention that since the Government had only recently declared that all independent schools should use their expertise to assist failing secondary schools, she was certain of highly favourable headlines in an assortment of national newspapers as well as a very useful financial reward.)

The Mole Hillers had stood out like sore thumbs among the self-confident, affluent students of Deepdale Hall and most of Emma's friends had pointedly ignored their existence. Even Emma, who prided herself on her ability to talk to anyone, realised on reflection that she could have been a bit more welcoming. So when she had overheard Mrs Goddard mentioning to the head of Sixth Form that Harriet Smith had been through 'a particularly trying time in the last few years' and muttering something about 'if you read it in a book, you would be hard pressed to believe it,' her curiosity had been aroused and she had decided that the poor girl needed befriending.

In the short time she had known her, she had discovered that Harriet, who was extremely pretty in a chubby, Rubens-maiden kind of way, was really very sweet. She was softly spoken, with the faintest Welsh lilt to her voice, and she had neither nose ring nor tattoo;

and her gorgeous chestnut hair did not come out of a bottle. Sadly, she had no self-confidence and wore clothes that were so last season. To her credit, she was hugely grateful to Emma for taking notice of her and was perfectly happy to answer all her questions. Within half an hour of their first meeting, she had discovered that Harriet had once been a pupil at Oak Lodge private school but, following family problems, she had left and gone to Mole Hill three years before.

'Problems?' Emma had rested a hand lightly on Harriet's arm to instil confidence and encourage her to spill the beans.

'We lost all our money,' Harriet had told her quite openly. 'My dad gambles. Big time. And when he loses, he drinks.' She sighed. 'And then Mum – well, because of all the stress, she's ended up in Lady Chichester Hospital.'

Emma had been very impressed by Harriet's honesty; most people would have stuck with the wayward father and avoided mentioning a mother in a psychiatric hospital.

'That must be hard for you,' Emma sympathised.

'Thank you.' It was the simple sincerity with which Harriet spoke that had made Emma's mind up. She might be poor, her jeans might be badly cut, but she had potential. All she needed was someone with style, savvy and street-cred to sort her out. Which was clearly why Fate had sent her to Emma's school.

She had meant to start at once with a makeover – but revision and exams had spoilt her good intentions and, since Harriet was doing environmental sciences and music, and Emma was studying psychology, art and business studies, they hadn't exchanged more than a few words for at least six weeks. Now was clearly the time to put that right.

'You're not going over, are you?' Serena demanded as Emma picked up her drink. 'She'll only want to tag on with us all evening and she is *so* boring.'

'You really think she'd choose to hang out with a snob like you?' Emma remarked, turning her back and heading over to where Harriet was sitting.

'Hi, Harriet, how are you?' As she squeezed into the seat next to her new friend, she realised the question was a pretty unnecessary one. Harriet had clearly been crying; a couple of crumpled tissues lay discarded on the table, the whites of her eyes were distinctly pink and she was staring miserably first at her watch and then at her mobile phone.

'What's happened? Has someone stood you up?'

'How did you know?' Harriet asked incredulously.

'Call it a wild guess,' Emma said, smiling. 'Come on – who is it?'

'Rob,' Harriet said, sniffing. 'The guy I told you about over lunch that day?'

'Did you?' Emma had no recollection of either a shared lunch or a love element in Harriet's life but didn't think this was the time to say so. 'I mean – yes, yes, Rob. And?'

'He was supposed to meet me here – well, at least I think it was here – at eight o'clock, or it could have been nine, but anyway . . .'

'You're sure his name is Rob?' Emma teased.

'Of course I am,' Harriet replied, missing the joke completely. 'We're – well, we're not anything really, well we are sort of . . .'

'OK,' Emma said, her patience finally beginning to run out. 'Give me your phone.'

She didn't wait for a response but picked up the bright pink mobile, scanned the phone book and gestured to Harriet.

'Is this him? Rob Martin?'

Harriet nodded. 'Yes, but what are you doing? You can't —'

'Watch me!' Emma replied sternly. She began keying in a message.

Am at Mango M's. R U coming? If not am going on 2 a party. Harriet.

She read the message back to Harriet.

'Emma, no, you can't . . .'

'Too late,' Emma announced cheerfully. 'Done it!'

'But I'm not going to a party—' Harriet began.

'No, but he doesn't know that,' Emma explained. 'You have to do this with guys – let them think that you've got better things to do than wait for them, right?'

Harriet chewed her lip and said nothing, eyeing her phone as if it was about to explode.

'So come on, tell me about him,' Emma said. 'What's he like? How long have you been an item? What's the low-down?'

'He's Libby's brother,' she said. 'Libby's my best friend – my only friend – at Mole Hill. She's doing media studies – you know, she's the one with the strawberry streak in her hair and the butterfly tattoo on her ankle?'

Bad start, thought Emma, but kept smiling encouragingly.

'I've been staying with her for a couple of weeks, ever since they repossessed our house . . .'

'What? Someone took your house away? Why?'

'It's what happens when your father doesn't pay the mortgage for months on end,' Harriet replied, ruefully. 'Libby's mum said I could sleep on the sofa bed till things got sorted. 'Course, Dad's doing his usual head-in-the-sand stuff and disappeared off to recoup his losses – which means he might win enough to rent somewhere for a month or so before he loses it all again at the races – and . . .'

'Harriet, that's awful.'

Emma was genuinely distressed. The thought of not having your own bedroom and bathroom and chilling-out space was just too horrific. So horrific she changed the subject.

'So you and Rob are an item?'

'Well, not an item, exactly,' Harriet admitted. 'I really like him and he told Libby he thought I was kinda cute and, the first night I was there, we went out in a foursome with Libby and her boyfriend.' She sighed. 'And then yesterday I went to the Sea Life Centre – that's where he's working for the summer – and he was there and he said "hi" and I said "hi" . . .'

Without doubt, thought Emma, their conversation would make the front page of the *Sun* seem intellectually challenging.

'And then he said let's meet for a drink on our own – he said "on our own", Emma, and that must mean . . .

well. Anyway, I said great, and he said – well, I think he said to come here tonight. But now I'm wondering whether it was somewhere else. See, I was so nervous . . .'

'Nervous? Of him?' Emma asked.

'No silly, I was nervous because I was there for an interview for a job. Only I didn't get it.'

It was as if a flash bulb had gone off in Emma's brain.

'A holiday job? For the summer? And you didn't get it?'

Watch it, she told herself sharply. You're starting to sound like her.

Harriet shook her head. 'They said I lacked experience. Which is true, but I so need the money.' She swallowed hard. 'Last week, I couldn't even afford to take Mum her favourite chocolate bar. And I've had to ditch my piano tuition. I'll do anything. Only jobs are thin on the ground. I guess I've left it too late.'

Emma thought fast. This was her chance: OK, so Harriet wasn't exactly overflowing with confidence and social graces but she'd be grateful and work hard; and, more importantly, Emma could help her get back with the sort of people she used to know before her useless father ruined her life.

'And you'd do anything? Like making beds? Or waitressing?' she asked eagerly.

'Sure, but I've tried all the hotels and they're full of Poles and Estonians who are there for the long haul,' Harriet said. 'The job I was after was perfect; it was in the gift shop at the Sea Life Centre. I wanted to be near Rob, you see.'

Her voice faded plaintively.

'Harriet, forget Rob. Forget the Sea Life Centre. Your problems are over.' She squeezed her friend's arm. 'How would you like . . .?' she began and then paused as Harriet's phone bleeped.

'It's him!' Harriet snatched the phone, scanned the message and then dropped it into her lap. Emma seized it.

Sorry. V. busy. Enjoy party. Rob.

One look at Harriet's distraught expression did away with the last vestige of doubts about her grand scheme. What Harriet needed was a fresh start with people who were clued up about priorities.

'How would you like a job somewhere really swish – and starting immediately?' she asked.

Harriet's pale blue eyes widened.

'It's at Donwell Abbey.' She paused, realising that someone like Harriet probably hadn't a clue what that was. 'It's a country house-hotel-type place in my village.' She paused as Harriet's chubby face turned pinker by the second. 'And forget sofa beds! You can stay at my house – it's next door to Donwell. And don't worry, you'd have your own room and bathroom.'

Harriet's mouth dropped open and Emma couldn't help thinking she resembled one of the fish in the Sea Life tanks.

'It's not mega bucks, but better than a lot of jobs and there are loads of perks,' she pressed on, assuming that money was, quite naturally, a major issue for her friend. 'And you'd get at least two days off a week so we could do loads of stuff together.' Like remodelling you, waving two fingers to your father . . . Emma thought.

Harriet clamped her hands to her mouth and stared at Emma.

'Harriet, there is just one condition to this job – you have to speak,' Emma teased. 'Yes or no?'

'Oh my God!' Harriet gasped. 'Me? With you?'

'Harriet!'

'Yes, yes, yes!' Harriet cried. 'I can't believe it! I mean, I've never been anywhere that posh in my entire life. Not even when we had money. No slot machines for Dad to bash, I guess,' she added with a sigh.

'Just keep that fact to yourself, OK?' Emma begged her. 'And do as I say, right?'

'Of course.' Harriet nodded eagerly. 'Just wait till I text Rob . . .'

'Harriet, no way!' Emma gasped. 'He has just stood you up – keep him guessing. Don't get in touch till he comes grovelling.'

'But what if he thinks I'm going to the party with a boy? What if —?'

'All the better,' Emma declared firmly. 'You mustn't be too available. Trust me, I know about these things.'

'Oh Emma, thank you, thank you.' Harriet's eyes were actually glistening with unshed tears and Emma felt a huge wave of compassion for her friend. mixed with the satisfaction that, yet again, her perception and charity was about to make life better for another human being.

Catching sight of Lucy and Adam entwined around one another on the dance floor, she smiled to herself. She'd done it before and she could do it again. Harriet didn't only deserve a decent summer job. She deserved to be rescued from the pit into which her father had cast her; she deserved more than a guy who put lobsters before love.

She made a vow there and then that, by the time the summer was over, Harriet's life would be changed for ever.

'So I'm off the hook? You won't keep looking at me like I've caused World War Three?' Lucy teased, after Harriet had left the club to go and tell Libby and her mum that she would be leaving and Emma had filled her in on the job situation.

'You're forgiven,' Emma said, smiling, still basking in the warm glow of doing a good turn. 'Harriet's a more deserving cause than you ever were.'

'Good,' Lucy replied. 'Because Adam and I need your help.'

'You didn't look as if you needed anyone's help a moment ago,' Emma said. 'Talk about full-on snogging.'

'Stop it!' Lucy blushed and glanced across to the bar where Adam was getting drinks. 'It's about Freddie.'

Instantly, Emma's brain went on to red alert.

'Freddie?' she repeated, trying not to look too interested. 'What about him?'

Freddie Churchill was Adam's half-brother but, unlike Adam, he was seriously A-list. His picture appeared in everything from *Cheerio!* to *Country Life*, and he was currently the face of Carstairs Countrywear. When Emma had first discovered the connection between him and Adam, she couldn't get her head around it; how come Freddie lived the high life twenty-four seven, while Adam was working all summer to keep his student loan at bay? It didn't make sense.

Lucy had quickly put her straight. Apparently, Adam's mum, Julia, had divorced Freddie's dad, the Churchill Chocolates' millionaire, way back when Freddie was two years old, and had married Sam Weston, a Cumbrian sheep farmer. (Why she would want to exchange three homes on two continents for a rambling farmhouse halfway up a windswept fell, Emma couldn't imagine. Lucy had muttered something about sexual chemistry and Emma not having a clue about the power of real love, but Emma had dismissed that as being sentimental rubbish that failed all the rules of logic.) Adam had been born alarmingly quickly after the marriage and, for reasons that Lucy hadn't found out, Freddie had gone to live with his father and been educated at one of the country's top public schools. Adam, meanwhile, had stayed with his mother and endured the mixed blessing of Kenworth Community College.

It had been the sudden death of the by then bankrupt sheep farmer, five years earlier, that had brought Adam and his mother to Sussex, where they lived for a while with Adam's grandmother, Thalia, who ran the Wealden Art Gallery in Emma's village and was the leading light of numerous good causes. Within a year of their arrival, Mrs Weston had found solace in the arms of an overweight American widower with a sad taste in ties and was now living in a condo in Winter Park, Florida, where she spent her time working out in pink Lycra and telling everyone to have a nice day. Adam, who, although he would never admit it, was something of a home-loving guy, had opted to remain in Sussex with his grandmother.

On the couple of occasions that Freddie had come to

Sussex to commiserate with Adam over their mother's bad taste in men, he had made a big impression on the girls in Emma's set: his languid good looks, easy manner and free use of cash made him the ideal catch. He flirted, he backchatted – but none of them managed to get a date out of him. Even Emma. And for someone who was used to being the centre of attention, the experience only served to make Freddie Churchill even more alluring than he might otherwise have been.

'So what's all this about Freddie?' Emma demanded the moment Adam appeared with drinks. 'Lucy said you needed my help.'

'OK, so how much do you know?' Adam asked. 'I mean, I guess Lucy told you about this massive twenty-first birthday party Freddie's dad had planned for him, right?'

'No,' Emma said, throwing Lucy a 'thanks so much for keeping me informed' look.

'Well, apparently Freddie's father had it all worked out,' Adam went on, just the faintest touch of envy in his voice. 'Black tie do at his villa in the South of France and then partying on his new yacht. You know what Freddie's father's like: fork out zillions and get everyone to grovel for an invitation. That was his big idea.'

'Was?' Emma queried.

Adam took a swig of his Budweiser.

'I don't know all the details,' he admitted. 'Freddie was so boiling mad when he phoned that he could hardly speak. I just gathered, between expletives, that they had a massive row – I don't know what about exactly – but it ended with Freddie telling his dad where to stuff his party and storming out. And guess what?'

'Go on,' Emma urged.

'Freddie says that he's sick to death of his father trying to control his life and that, since Granny and I are the only sane members of the family, he's coming to Brighton to hang out for the summer!'

Emma and Lucy exchanged glances. The note of pride in Adam's voice was unmistakable. Emma understood immediately; she had just finished reading *So Love Me – A Study of Separated Siblings* as part of her pre-uni reading list and realised that Adam was craving acceptance and recognition from his big brother. His next remark confirmed her suspicions.

'He's really rebelling,' Adam went on admiringly. 'He's even decided to celebrate his birthday down here – whatever his father thinks.'

'Backlash against parental control,' Emma murmured knowledgeably.

'Whatever.' Adam continued. 'He wants just his best mates – nothing huge and showy, and definitely no interfering parents. Not even Mum. And he says, if I help him sort it, I can invite some of my mates, too.'

He flung an arm around Lucy's sunburnt shoulders and hugged her to him.

'Brilliant! That is so cool!' Emma said, her mind racing ahead.

'But if his dad's not footing the bill . . .?' Lucy began.

'No problem,' Adam said, shrugging. 'Freddie's got a pile of money from when his dad's mother died as well as from all the advertising he does. He's going to stay with

Granny for a bit – he can have my room while I'm at the Frontier Adventure Centre – but then he's even talking about taking a flat in town and you don't get those for peanuts.'

'So when's he coming?' Emma asked eagerly, mentally booking in highlights, a facial and some serious clothes shopping into her schedule.

'Oh, you know Freddie,' Adam said. 'He says . . .'

'Hey, did I hear you talk about Freddie? Freddie Churchill?' Tabitha sashayed up to them. 'Is he here?' Her eyes scanned the club like a sparrowhawk looking for a choice mouse.

'No, he's not.' Emma shook her head. 'And, as a matter of interest, do you make a habit of bursting in on private conversations?'

'He's coming down some time next week,' Adam told her innocently, clearly mesmerised by Tabitha's cleavage. 'He's doing a series of fashion shoots for *Country Matters* magazine – Ashdown Forest, Cuckmere Haven, all over the place.'

'Cool,' Tabitha remarked. 'Just let me know when he's around, Adam, right? He is seriously hot.'

'That girl,' muttered Emma, as Tabitha turned away and grabbed the arm of Simon Wittering, 'is a menace. So this party – what's the low-down?'

'Freddie wants me and Lucy to suss out some party venues so he can check them out when he gets here. Like, who does he think I am? Superman? It'll be impossible – everything will be booked solid.'

He downed the final dregs of his drink.

'He's got this idea of finding a place where his mates

can stay and make a weekend of it. Freddie never did anything by halves. He wants golf and tennis and . . .'

'I thought you said he didn't want anything showy,' Lucy interrupted.

'By Freddie's standards, it's not,' Adam said. 'It's the country life thing he wants, you know with his advertising image and everything.'

'That's it! Oh my God, Adam, that's it! Donwell. It's perfect.'

'Donwell?' Adam repeated, in that blank way that guys have when faced with a new idea that they haven't had three hours to process. 'How do you mean, Donwell?'

Ten minutes later, having extolled the virtues of croquet on the lawn, easy access to the club scene in Brighton, clay pigeon shooting up the road and a huge party on The Day, Emma had them both convinced.

'But a place like that'll be booked solid,' Adam groaned. 'His birthday's only three weeks away.'

'I have contacts,' Emma assured him, not wanting to let on that the place was half empty and she wasn't actually pulling strings. 'Just leave it with me. I'll get back to you after the weekend. You email Freddie and let him know I'm on the case.'

❧ CHAPTER 3 ❧

Secret scheme:
Finding a friend a love life without lobsters

'I WAS WONDERING,' HARRIET SAID THE FOLLOWING DAY, 'could we just pop into the Sea Life Centre? You could meet Rob.'

Emma was about to say that, after three hours of shopping in Brighton in an attempt to give Harriet a new image on a minimal budget, she was more inclined to slump down in Café Caprice with a large latte and a chocolate brownie than endure the subterranean world of electric eels and basking sharks; but she was well aware that, despite all her instructions, Harriet wouldn't relax until she'd seen Rob; and, having spent ages on the telephone that morning convincing George that Harriet was an absolute find, far more hardworking than Lucy and he was lucky to get her, she felt she had to do all she could to ensure that her friend arrived at Donwell in a calm and serene frame of mind. There was a first time for everything.

Besides, she felt she owed it to Harriet – she was still smarting from the conversation that had taken place in the middle of High Wire, the funky new designer boutique in Regent Arcade. Harriet had proved to be surprisingly quick to learn how to choose outfits, matching and contrasting colours and finding accessories. Which made it all the more surprising that her clothes were so, well, ordinary.

'So go on, try them on!' Emma had urged.

'Get real,' Harriet had said calmly. 'No way could I afford this lot. What I do is find what I like and then hunt through the market and the charity shops for lookalikes.'

Emma had managed to hide her inclination to shudder. The thought of wearing clothes that other people had perspired in was beyond her wildest comprehension.

'OK, so just get one outfit,' Emma had encouraged her, grabbing a selection of clothes. 'See, this lot would be under a hundred pounds.'

Harriet had stared at her. 'You don't get it, do you?' she had said, shaking her head. 'I don't have anywhere near that kind of money. Not any more.'

It was that last phrase that did it for Emma. That anyone should be made to go without the latest fashion, just because her father was a total waster, was just not on.

'OK,' she had said, linking her arm through Harriet's. 'Tell you what – I'll buy these for you. Call it an early birthday pressie.'

'No! My birthday's not till November and besides, I couldn't – I mean, no way – you hardly know me . . . that amount of money . . .'

'And what's more,' Emma had gone on, 'when we get to my place, we'll go through my wardrobe. I've loads of stuff I don't wear and even though you are a bit bigger than me . . .'

'Like two sizes!'

'. . . I'm sure we can find some stuff,' Emma had concluded, even though she wasn't sure at all. It just made her feel good to try.

'But I can't pay you back . . . I don't know what to say . . .'

'So don't say a thing!' Emma had declared, tossing her charge card at the assistant. 'Just enjoy!'

Now, trekking down East Street and along the Seafront, thronging with holidaymakers, she was enjoying the warm glow that being charitable always induced in her. She even bought a copy of the *Big Issue* from a guy in a bookshop doorway, just to ensure that the feeling lasted a little longer.

As they reached the entrance of the Sea Life Centre, she gasped. 'Eight pounds fifty!' she muttered, gesturing to the board at the doorway. 'I'm not paying that just for you to chat up this guy.'

Clothes spending was one thing. Paying the price of a lip liner to gaze at jellyfish? No way. She turned to go.

'We won't have to pay,' Harriet said proudly, fumbling in her bag and pulling out a plastic pass. 'They gave me a free pass – consolation for not getting the job. It's valid till tomorrow and it admits two people. So come on!'

Emma followed her into the vaulted Victorian aquarium.

'There he is! That's him – over there. Isn't he gorgeous?'

Emma blinked, her eyes adjusting to the dim lighting, and glanced across the concourse to where a crowd of children were peering into a huge Touch Pool. A stockily built guy wearing a fluorescent yellow jacket was holding a rather angry-looking lobster in one hand and a very prickly starfish in the other. Since there was no one else over the age of ten in sight, Emma assumed that he must be Harriet's idea of fit.

'Hi, Rob!' Emma cringed as Harriet waved frantically in an attempt to attract his attention. For a second, Rob looked up, coloured and turned away.

'He didn't see me,' Harriet began.

'I think he did,' Emma said, grabbing her arm before she could wave again. 'He's working. Come on, let's go.'

Sadly, at that very moment, the cluster of children began to disperse and Rob, having put the lobster and starfish gently back into the pool, spoke briefly to a tall man with a clipboard and then turned and beckoned surreptitiously to Harriet.

'Coming!' Harriet broke into a run and dashed over to him.

Emma hung back but, when she realised she couldn't hear a word they were saying, she began to drift towards them, feigning huge interest in a tank of stingrays and an exhibit marked *The Romance of the Rock Pool*.

'I can't, Harriet, not now, I'll get into trouble,' she heard Rob say.

Harriet looked as if she was about to burst into tears. Emma watched as Rob glanced at his watch.

'But next Thursday – I've got a day off . . .' he began.

She caught the words 'job' and 'Donwell with Emma'

from Harriet, and edged nearer. She wondered just what it was that her friend found attractive about the guy: he was only an inch or so taller than Harriet, had the sort of nose that looked as if it had lost out to the All Blacks, and, whereas Harriet had a very attractive voice, Rob's accent was very definitely South London.

'This is my friend, Emma,' Harriet told him. 'She's the one who got me the job.'

'Hey, that's cool,' Rob replied, smiling broadly at Emma. 'So you're the one to get Harry time off on Thursday, right?'

'Wrong,' Emma cut in quickly, wincing at the nickname while smiling sweetly through clenched teeth. 'It's a really full-on job; there won't be any time off for at least a week.'

And by then, I'll have made sure that Harriet has far more exciting things to do than spend time with a guy who wears cords and smells of gone-off herring, she thought.

'No probs,' he shrugged, turning back to Harriet. 'Tell you what, babe, I'll call you, OK? Got to go – the big boss says I can have a go at the penguin feeding.'

'Really?' Emma murmured, trying for Harriet's sake to sound interested.

'Oh yes, it's fascinating,' Rob replied eagerly. 'They have these spiny tongues and, of course, they have this distinct hierarchy – even in captivity, the older ones get to feed first.'

'Oh my goodness, is that the time? My parking ticket runs out in five minutes!' Emma exclaimed. Politeness was one thing; dying of boredom quite another.

Much as she thought Rob was a loser, Emma couldn't help feeling sorry for Harriet, whose lips were still puckered in anticipation of a kiss as he disappeared through the door with an airy wave and no backward glance.

'He's lovely, isn't he?' Harriet asked eagerly as they walked back to Emma's car.

Rather than lie, Emma found herself assailed by a fit of sneezing, hoping that Harriet would take the jerking of her head as a nod.

❧ CHAPTER 4 ❧

Daring dream:
To win the crown of party planner/matchmaker of the year

'EMMA! OH MY GOD, EMMA – LOOK!'

As Emma manoeuvred her bright red Daihatsu Charade into the drive on Saturday afternoon, and pulled up outside her own front door she smiled, just a little wearily, at yet another of Harriet's verbal explosions. She had been ooh-ing and aah-ing ever since Emma had picked her up from her friend's rather run-down semi in Hollyhill, one of Brighton's less attractive areas. First, it was the 'amazing' and 'dinky' little car that had been Emma's seventeenth birthday present from her father (when Emma switched on the ignition and the message 'Hello, Happy' appeared on the instrument display, Harriet went into paroxysms of unrestrained glee); this was followed by a seemingly endless reading and re-reading of two text messages from Rob both of which, as Harriet kept telling her, had three x's at the end and that must mean he loves her right? – and now there was another exclamation of astonishment, the source of which Emma couldn't fathom.

'That man, Emma – over there. It's him!'

Emma glanced to the left where a figure in ill-fitting trousers and a pork-pie hat was striding purposefully along the gravel path towards the orchard.

'So? What about it?'

'What about it?' Harriet repeated. 'Emma, are you blind? That's Tarquin Tee – the guy off the telly. The one who does *Going Green*, the one with —'

'OK, OK, I don't need a potted biography of my own father,' Emma said, pulling up outside the front door.

'Your . . . you mean . . . but he can't . . .' Harriet stammered and then turned and glared at Emma accusingly. 'He's your *dad*? How come you never told me?'

Emma shrugged. 'I never thought,' she admitted, switching off the ignition and releasing her seat belt. 'All my mates know and I guess I just – well, I assumed you did too.'

By now, Harriet's nose was glued to the car window.

'Will I get to talk to him?' she asked in breathy tones.

'Oh no,' Emma replied sarcastically. 'You'll be staying in our house but, of course, a word won't pass his lips! Of course you'll get to talk to him, silly. Although whether he'll have anything riveting to say is quite another matter.'

As if he had heard her, Tarquin turned, put a hand in front of his eyes to shield them from the glare of the sun, and began beckoning wildly.

'Looks as if your moment has come,' Emma teased, opening the car door. 'Only please, don't drool for too long; it's bad for his ego and, besides, we're going to dump your stuff and then go round to George's. I've got things to sort.'

'This is so amazing, I can't get my head round it. Oh my God!' Harriet kept saying, clearly far more impressed by Emma's balding father than the upcoming social event of the season.

'Emma darling, perfect timing!' Tarquin cried. 'And you must be Harriet – welcome to Hartfield!'

'Hello, I'm really – I mean it's so good of you – and the programme . . . I just love it . . . and I'm really into conservation and . . .'

Fortunately, Tarquin was too buzzed up to listen to Harriet's stammering.

'Now, Emma, listen,' he enthused. 'I've had the most brilliant idea!'

Emma groaned inwardly. When inspiration struck her father, it was usually of two kinds: either highly embarrassing, involving her in making excuses for why everyone had received shapeless Fair Trade cotton T-shirts or Make Your Own Log kits for Christmas; or very labour intensive, with her as the labour.

'It came to me in the shower,' her father went on. 'You know George is in a state about the new bedrooms not being ready? Well, his worries are over – he can put some of the guests in my lodges. Be great publicity for me and the TV programmers will love it.'

Emma hesitated. 'What does George think about it?'

'Bit doubtful,' Tarquin admitted. 'Anyone would think I was suggesting putting them in mud huts.'

Emma was hardly surprised. Her father was the first man in the South of England to build eco-lodges; they were little two-room earth shelters, built into the side of the hill at the bottom of their orchard, their roofs covered with plants and grass. They reminded Emma of Teletubby houses, but the BBC were fascinated and were devoting a whole episode of *Going Green* to what they called 'Down to Earth – the New Way of Living' – but then they weren't aspirational guests forced to give up power showers, surround sound TV and the newest version of in-room coffee maker for the privilege.

'Perhaps,' she suggested, 'the film crew could stay there? Or maybe you should just pretend someone was there? I could pose for them – that way there won't be other people's mess lying around.'

'Now that *is* an idea! You'd be perfect,' Tarquin exclaimed, turning to Harriet. 'Isn't she a clever girl? Of course, her mother was very inventive, God rest her soul.'

His eyes took on the faraway look that Emma knew was a warning of worse to come.

'OK, Harriet, let's get going,' Emma butted in firmly. The last thing she needed was for her father to go into one of his maudlin phases right now. 'I'll show you where you're sleeping and then we must go. I promised George that I'd get you over there in time to help in the tearoom.'

'Lily can do teas,' Tarquin interrupted. 'She's going to be a sort of general dogsbody to Mrs P and this Italian chap, just till things calm down a bit.'

'Lily?' Emma gasped. 'You don't mean to tell me George has actually asked Lily Bates to work there?'

Her father shook his head. 'Not George – it was my

other bright idea,' he said proudly. 'Now she's at catering college, she needs all the experience she can get. And it'll be fun for her – heaven knows, she deserves some.'

For the second time that day, Emma felt a pang of conscience. Lily's mum had for many years been their housekeeper but, when Emma was ten, Mrs Bates was diagnosed with multiple sclerosis and her condition had deteriorated so fast that she was now wheelchair bound. Tarquin had installed them in a cottage in the village and paid their rent, but it was Lily, an only child, who had grown up caring for her mum, combining school and homework with household chores, shopping and cooking. She had never had much of a social life and was, in Emma's opinion, totally without the social skills necessary to ever get one.

'Can't I just see the lodges?' Harriet pleaded, finally managing to string an entire sentence together. 'Have they got sedum roofs? I read a book about earth sheltering when I did my GCSE rural studies course.'

'You did? This is wonderful – Emma's totally switched off from the whole thing. Come along, I'll show you,' Tarquin said. 'You see, contrary to what people believe, they are full of light; I've used glass on one side and . . .'

To Emma's relief, her father's mobile phone rang at that moment. He snatched it from his pocket and closed his eyes, a habit he always had when speaking on the phone.

'What? It's not? You haven't? They didn't?' Tarquin's face was growing more purple by the second. 'Give me ten minutes and I'll be there.'

'Problem?' Emma asked.

'Our local MP has just flown – *flown*, mind you – from Shoreham Airport to Exeter for a seminar. And he's the one who goes on about carbon footprints. Davina and I are heading for the *Evening Argus* right now – I want headlines in tomorrow's edition, I want . . .'

What else he wanted Emma didn't discover as he was already out of earshot, heading for the office above the garage where Davina, his personal assistant, was undoubtedly already scribbling a suitable invective for his next press release.

'Sorry about that,' Emma said. 'When Dad's on one of his rants, there's no stopping him.'

'He is,' Harriet sighed, 'absolutely lovely. You are so lucky to have a dad like that.'

'You mean one that goes round switching off lights and wearing slightly grubby shirts because he won't let anyone wash at more than thirty degrees? That kind of lucky?'

'No,' Harriet said solemnly. 'A dad that hasn't gambled your home away. That kind of lucky.'

Emma said nothing. She felt too ashamed.

'Oh wow! It's amazing!' Harriet stood open-mouthed outside the front door of Donwell Abbey, her eyes scanning from the immaculate lawns, fringed with beech, sycamore and Scots pines and staked out with archery targets to the shimmering waters of the spa pool, glimpsed through the window of what had once been the orangery.

Emma had to admit that, despite knowing the house almost as well as her own, she never failed to be impressed by its russet walls, almost hidden under great swathes of Virginia creeper, its numerous mullioned windows that twinkled when they caught the late afternoon sun, and the vast oak front door with its enormous lion's head door knocker.

'I can't wait to see inside!' Harriet bounded ahead of Emma up the stone steps just as the front door opened and a cascade of croquet mallets and hoops hurtled down the steps.

'Oh ****!' A broad-shouldered, dark-haired guy with the faintest hint of designer stubble lunged towards Harriet, almost knocking her off her feet.

'Oh sorry,' he gasped. 'Look, can you hang on to these for a second?'

He thrust a box of croquet balls into her arms and began scooping up the hoops scattered over the steps. As he stood up, he caught sight of Emma and promptly dropped them again.

'Hi, Theo – clumsy as ever I see!' Emma laughed. 'I didn't expect to find you here.' She turned to Harriet. 'This is Theo Elton, famous for asking me to dance at the South Downs Ball and totally ruining my Manolo Blahniks. And that was before he fell into the water feature.'

Theo broke into a grin and pulled a face. 'Thank you for that, Emma!' He winked at her. 'I'm glad I made such an impression. Hey, you've cut your hair short.'

Emma was so gob-smacked that a guy would notice such a thing that she completely failed to reply with a witty riposte. She'd known Theo, who was studying medicine at Cambridge, for years; he had grown up in the neighbouring village of Fyfield. His father was chaplain of Fyfield College, which was only half a notch lower than Eton and Harrow in the swank ratings and the Knightley boys had been at school with him. Theo had always seemed a bit of an oddball; an only child whose idea of fun was playing in chess tournaments and keeping geckos. But now, as she eyed his tanned legs in frayed denim shorts and noted the way his slate-grey eyes crinkled at the edges when he smiled, she realised that he'd turned into someone almost worthy of a place on her reserve list for parties.

'Look, I know you've only just got here,' Theo ventured. 'But you couldn't help me set up the croquet on the lawn, could you? A couple of the guests want to play and they are most definitely not the type to be kept waiting.'

'Well, not really because I need to see George about something vital,' Emma began.

He sighed. 'Don't talk to me about George! He gets me over here to revamp the hotel website and what do I end up doing? Acting as some kind of unpaid groundsman!' He looked at the clutter of croquet equipment in disgust.

'I'll help you,' Harriet offered eagerly. 'Not that I have a clue what to do.'

'I'll show you,' Theo assured her. 'You're a star – thanks a lot.' He gathered up the kit and headed towards the manicured upper lawn. 'Follow me!'

Emma watched them as they began hammering hoops

into the lawn, Theo's muscular arms swinging in even strokes while Harriet wielded the mallet as if it might explode in her hands at any minute. She smiled to herself as Theo marched purposefully behind Harriet, and put his hands over hers, demonstrating just how it should be done. And, as Harriet turned and smiled up into Theo's face, the seed of an idea began sprouting in Emma's fertile imagination.

George's father had been adamant that his home should look like a home and not be, in his words, 'tarted up and commercialised'. As a result, there were none of the trappings of the usual bland hotel. The ten guest bedrooms had names instead of numbers, the sitting rooms were often frequented by the family dogs, Breeze, Brenna and Brodie, and the games room still housed the table tennis table and Subbuteo that Emma and George had fought over as children, along with piles of board games and an ancient Bagatelle. The reception desk just inside the front door was an old pine table, and behind it was a tiny office – once a walk-in closet – from where Emma could hear the odd 'Damn!' and 'Oh, sugar!' being muttered. She punched the bell, winced slightly at the 'Now what?' grunted from behind the half-open office door, and then grinned as George burst out, looking anything but the welcoming host.

'Oh, it's you. Am I glad to see you!' He gave Emma a quick hug and glanced around the hall, its walls festooned with portraits of somewhat severe Knightleys of old. 'Where's this Harriet person? Don't tell me she's dropped out as well,' he groaned.

'She's in the garden helping Theo with the croquet stuff,' Emma said.

'Already? Good on her.' He nodded approvingly.

'You didn't tell me he'd be here.'

George shrugged. 'To be honest, it was a spur of the moment kind of thing after we'd had a few beers at the cricket club last Wednesday. I was saying what a mess the website was in – as if I didn't have enough problems – and I asked if he felt like helping me out, seeing as how he's so into all that technical stuff.'

'Good idea.'

'Well, he wasn't exactly smitten with the idea at first, but I said you and Lucy would be here, and there'd be the chance to play golf and use the health club.'

'Bribery!'

'I just thought it might cheer him up. Verity Price chucked him last month and he's taken it really badly.' He chuckled. 'Do you know, she was his first ever girlfriend? Can you believe that? What's he been doing all this time?'

Seeing the look of disbelief on her friend's face, Emma wondered fleetingly how many girlfriends George had had. With his olive skin and eyes the colour of overcooked gingerbread, he wasn't bad looking, and, when he was in the right mood, he could charm the birds off the trees. He had been at uni for three years, and most of his holidays had been spent on work experience projects in America and France; she'd hardly seen anything of him until this summer. He could have been doing anything.

'So he's unattached? Available?' Emma asked eagerly.

'Oh, come off it – he is *so* not your type,' George responded at once. 'He has a brilliant brain but . . .'

'Oh? And I don't?'

'Let's put it this way – he uses his for things other than shopping, reading fashion magazines and interfering in people's lives.'

'I'll have you know that my interfering, as you so inappropriately call it, has made a lot of people very happy. And as for me being interested in Theo – get real! I've better things to do with my time.'

'Good! And the first thing can be making up beds. Or doing the flower arrangements for the dining room. Which do you want?'

'Hang on, I'm doing the hostess bit,' she reminded him. 'No way am I changing other people's sheets.'

'For God's sake, Emma!' George snapped back. 'Can we get one thing straight, OK? My back's really to the wall here and if you're not going to pitch in and get on with things, you might as well go home now.'

'Speak to me like that and I just might,' Emma retorted. 'We're not kids any more –you can't just boss me about.'

'Actually, that is exactly what I can do,' George assured her. 'Till Mum and Dad get back, they've put me in charge, whether you like it or not.'

'Well, I don't —'

'And neither do I as it happens. I didn't ask to spend my time dealing with a load of guests who all expect to be treated like VIPs and worrying myself sick about my parents and their total ineptitude.'

Emma felt rather small and very guilty. Suddenly it was as if there was more than four and half years separating them, as if George had turned all responsible and mature while he'd been away and she was doing what she'd always done as a kid – sulking until she got her own way.

'I'm sorry,' she said, touching George's arm lightly. 'I'm useless at flowers so I guess if I have to do beds . . . ' She shuddered at the mere thought.

'Thanks.' George ran a hand through his dishevelled curls and Emma smiled at the memory of George, aged fourteen, trying desperately to flatten them with half a pot of hair gel. 'I didn't mean to go off on one – it's just that I've had Mum on the phone howling her eyes out . . .'

'Your dad's not worse?' Emma gasped.

'No, actually he's fully conscious now, and sitting up demanding a Scotch.'

'That's wonderful!'

'Mmm,' murmured George, 'except that, while he was concussed, he kept calling Mum Polly and saying she was a hot little sexpot. The doctors say it's quite usual to get confused after a bash on the head, but Mum is seriously not amused.' He grinned at her, and she saw a glimpse of the old, flippant George. 'What's more,' he said smiling, 'she's spoken to your father and now she seems to think that having you around will be an asset to this place. Must be her brain that's affected, not Dad's!' Come on, I'll get you a uniform.'

'Uni—' Emma was about to stipulate quite emphatically that no way was she about to cover up her Armani jeans with some tacky two-piece but remembered that she had more important things to discuss.

'George,' she said sweetly. 'Hang on a minute. How would you like to make some serious money for your parents and get this establishment on to the Top Ten Must Visit list?'

'Oh yeah? And what Fairy Godmother is going to make that happen?' George replied sarcastically.

'Me,' smiled Emma. 'Now, just listen . . .'

It took a full ten minutes, but somehow Emma managed to move George on from, 'Freddie Churchill? As in the Chocolates people? Don't be ridiculous!' through, 'But Emma we can't do it – it's way out of our league' to a much more satisfying, 'I suppose it wouldn't do any harm to find out what he wants.'

'Of course it wouldn't,' Emma said decisively. 'Just think of the publicity. And I'll do all the planning and Harriet and Lily . . .'

'Can do all the hard graft,' muttered George. 'Typical you.'

'Do you mind?' Emma protested. 'You've got two weeks with only a few bookings, I've just found you a real gold mine – that lot will spend zillions on booze and stuff and you've got the marquee you use for weddings – and now you're slagging me off.'

George's face broke into a grin. 'OK, point taken,' he conceded. 'And I doubt very much that Freddie will want to come here anyway – he's more an Arundel Castle or Royal Pavilion type.' He chewed his lip. 'But, I'd better clear it with the parents, just in case. I may be the only one with any vision in this family, but they do

T038276

own the place. What time is it in Cape Town?'

Emma was about to follow him into the office, in case the Knightleys needed any added encouragement, when Theo burst into the hall. 'Croquet up and running and the Frobishers are all set to whack the hell out of one another,' he announced with a laugh.

'Where's Harriet?' Emma asked.

'Making a phone call,' he replied. 'She said she couldn't get a mobile signal inside the house and there was someone she was desperate to contact.'

'I can guess who.' Emma sighed. 'Oh dear.'

'Problem? She did seem a bit anxious.'

Theo was looking intently at her. Thanks to what she had just learned from George, the idea that had flashed through Emma's mind earlier took on a whole new dimension.

'Harriet has had such tragedy in her life,' she began. 'And I'm really worried about her.' She paused, gratified to see that she had Theo's complete attention. 'I can't say any more because it's all too awful. It was so good of you to let her help because . . .' She dropped her voice conspiratorially. '. . . She really needs to learn to trust guys again.' She clamped a hand to her mouth theatrically. 'I've said too much – I just guess all we can do is be really kind to her and make sure she doesn't get into the wrong sort of set – she's been mixing with some really odd types, which is so sad because she's a lovely person but ever so vulnerable psychologically, if you know what I mean?' she concluded, reciting verbatim lines from *My Shadow Self* starring Kim Clayson.

Theo nodded earnestly. Emma reckoned that anyone

planning to be a doctor had to be hugely compassionate and understanding and, with a bit of luck, she could milk that attribute to Harriet's advantage.

'So what exactly happened to her?' Theo asked, edging closer to Emma and putting a hand on her arm. 'Is there anything I can do?'

'I can't break a confidence but, well, just make her feel one of us, I guess. It would really take a weight off my mind to know that someone else was looking out for her apart from me. Perhaps you could, like, chat to her . . . see if she'll open up. And don't let on I said anything. Promise?'

'Don't worry.' Theo nodded, speaking more softly, as George reappeared. 'You can rely on me.'

'Thanks.'

'So,' he said, turning to George, 'I'll see you later – I'm just going to nip into town.'

'You can't,' George cried. 'Not till you've sorted that bloody computer – it's eaten all the menu plans for Sunday.'

Theo raised his eyebrows and sighed. 'Computers don't eat stuff,' he replied, flexing his shoulders and brushing a hand across his perspiring forehead. 'Honestly George, for someone doing an MBA you are a total dinosaur when it comes to technology.'

Emma smiled to herself. It was true; George was old-fashioned, but in a nice way. He could be pompous (he'd once laid into Emma for getting caught on camera at Jasper Greenhill's eighteenth with her knickers showing – as if she'd known that *Sussex Scene* would print it with the caption *Tee's Teasing Teenager*) and he certainly had bizarre interests (fly-fishing in icy cold water and drag hunting in the pouring rain for starters), but he didn't follow the herd – he was his own man and he always said what he thought. She liked that in a guy.

'Well anyway, if we're going to host this party . . .'

'Party?' Theo raised an eyebrow and listened with increasing amusement as George told him about Freddie and confirmed that Mrs Knightley thought it was a wonderful idea and she'd been nagging Max to bring in the young set for ages.

'Which is fine, except that she's not here and if the whole thing goes pear-shaped and we're blacklisted by the cognoscenti . . .'

'Don't you mean glitterati?' Emma interjected.

'Whatever,' George snapped. 'Still, Freddie might not want to come, of course.'

'It sounds great,' Theo said. 'Not that I'll get invited. I don't even know the guy, although I know someone who does . . .'

''Course you'll come,' Emma cut in swiftly, before he had the chance to get all maudlin about Verity. 'I'll make sure of that.'

'Cool.' Theo grinned. 'Now if you don't mind, I'll find these lost menus.'

'And after you've sorted all that, I don't suppose you fancy a bit of flower arranging?' George teased as Theo headed for the office.

'Too right I don't,' Theo replied, holding up his hands and backing off. 'I'm out of here before you get any more dumb ideas!'

'Did you say flower arranging?' Harriet, flushed and smiling from ear to ear, came running into the hall. 'I'll do it – I love that kind of stuff.'

'You do? Sorry – you must be Harriet – I'm George.'

Harriet smiled nervously at George, and twiddled a strand of her curly chestnut hair round her finger.

'Thank you so much for giving me this job,' she enthused. 'I'm so excited I could burst. So where do I go?'

'I'll show you round the place and then take you to the flower room,' George said. 'Em, you know where to get the clean bedding, yeah? In the linen cupboard on the landing, right?'

This, thought Emma as she stomped upstairs, is so not the way it should be. Harriet ought to be stripping beds and I should be doing the upfront stuff, interacting with guests, gliding round the sitting room with a silver tray of canapés . . .

'Ah, at last! I've been ringing Reception for ten minutes – it simply isn't good enough!' A broad-shouldered, bald-headed man was standing on the landing, hands on hips. 'I ordered afternoon tea half an hour ago – where the hell is it?'

Like I should know, Emma thought. 'I am so sorry,' she replied, flashing him what she hoped was an understanding, slightly sexy, yet totally deferential, smile. 'We have had a few staff problems, which is why I've been called in to sort things out. Now, if you could just tell me your exact order, I'll see to it that it is dealt with immediately.'

'Hmm, well, that sounds more promising,' he grunted,

kicking open the door to his room and gesturing to Emma to come in. 'Check with my wife what it was she ordered – damned woman changes her mind like the wind.'

Five minutes later, having complimented Mrs Dalrymple on her delightful cashmere cardigan and agreed that there was nothing to beat a cup of Earl Grey and a lightly buttered scone in the afternoon, and yes, she was a cut above your usual young person, Emma knew she had found her niche in the hospitality business.

'Delightful girl,' murmured Colonel Dalrymple as she was leaving the room. 'What is your name, dear?'

'Emma Woodhouse, Guest Relations Manager,' she said. 'Anything you need during your stay, just come to me.'

By nine-thirty that evening, Emma had begun to realise that, rather than working her socks off for an advertising agency in London, her true vocation was to be a party planner to the stars. Or maybe a life coach to the upper classes. Or both. Solving other people's problems was so hugely satisfying.

In the space of three hours, she had introduced the Mulligans, who were desperate to learn croquet, to the Frobishers who spent the entire evening meal expounding the finer points of the game in ringing tones to anyone who would listen; told George that he must start serving high teas to the under-eights in order to avoid a repetition of little Phoebe Pilkington crawling under tables and throwing up over Colonel Dalrymple's

Crockett and Jones brogues, and given the teenage Mapperley twins not only a list of the best clubs in Brighton but phoned the taxi company for them and spent five minutes assuring their over-anxious mother that Brighton was not a den of vice and iniquity and that Fiona and Hamish would be quite safe.

'You're good at this ego-massaging bit, aren't you?' Theo commented, overhearing this last exchange as he emerged from the kitchen having scrounged some left-over pavlova. 'And you know, that idea of stuff for teens – I ought to put info like that on the website. You wouldn't believe how dull it is at the moment – all tariffs, menus and a boring bit about the Knightley history. Hardly likely to attract anyone under the age of fifty.'

'Go for it,' Emma encouraged, clearing coffee cups on to the trolley. 'Drag the place into the twenty-first century.'

'We have to do something,' he said with a laugh. 'If Freddie's guests check out this place on the web, they'll decide they'd rather watch paint dry than party here!'

Emma frowned. 'So what are you suggesting?'

'I don't know,' he mused. 'Something vibrant and upbeat. We can't put photos of real guests on the website – data protection and all that – but I was thinking we could use us lot instead. You'd be up for it, wouldn't you?'

'Sure,' Emma said. 'Provided I get to be the one who sips the champagne!'

'We'll get George, of course, and Lily . . .' He began scribbling on a notepad. 'And I thought you and me could hit the clubs in town, take some pictures and show what's on offer.'

'And take Harriet – she's dead photogenic,' Emma added.

'OK, that's a cool idea,' Theo agreed. 'Like you said – make her feel one of the crowd.'

'Brilliant.' Emma smiled smugly to herself. 'Why don't you ask her now? She's in the conservatory doing something interesting with a couple of fir cones.'

'Oh Emma, there you are. Oh, sorry – you're just leaving, right?'

Emma nodded, smiled wearily at Lily Bates and glanced rather pointedly at her watch.

'I won't keep you a minute – I mean, I should have asked you earlier, only what with the teas, and then Luigi letting me make the hollandaise sauce all on my own, and dashing back to the cottage to get Mum some supper – she's feeling really rough today so I did her smoked salmon and scrambled egg, she loves that, a bit of a luxury but once in while . . .'

'So, what was it you wanted?' Emma broke in, forcing a smile.

The instant the words were out, she regretted it. Looking at Lily, with her bony frame, pale face and grey eyes with permanent shadows circling them, one might have thought she suffered from some rather awful disease. In fact, she was bursting with health and energy, and the only condition from which she suffered was a bad case of verbal diarrhoea.

'Well, you see, the thing is, it's about Jake. You

remember Jake? Jake Fairfax? My cousin? The one . . .'

'. . . who is very musical, the one in the band,' Emma finished, suppressing a sigh as she recalled the interminable reports every few months about how amazing Split Bamboo was. 'Yes, I remember. What about him?'

'You'll never guess, not in a million years . . .'

'So perhaps if you told me . . .'

'What? Oh yes – sorry! Well, he's coming to Brighton. For four weeks! And guess why?'

'Haven't a clue.' Emma sighed.

'The band are playing at The Jacaranda Tree. And somewhere else I forget the name of. They've been booked for a whole month, two nights a week in each place. Isn't that amazing?'

'Yes, it is,' Emma admitted. She had always dismissed the band's reported success as being a figment of Lily's overactive imagination, but The Jacaranda Tree had built its reputation on showcasing upcoming chart-toppers and certainly weren't likely to book no-hopers.

'We wanted him to stay with us – Mum loves to have visitors – but he said no, that wouldn't do because the rest of the band are looking for lodgings too, so I said there's Mrs Butler's B & B in the village and he said he'd think about it, but to be honest he's in such a state at the moment . . .'

'Right, well . . .'

'You see, he broke up with Caroline. Oh, you don't know Caroline – she is – was – his girlfriend. Ever so nice, she and I got on really well. She's at Cambridge University, dead clever. She's doing politics and something or other. Anyway, she dumped him all of a sudden, just like that. I can't think why, because Jake's lovely and if we weren't cousins I could fancy him myself! What was I going to say?' She frowned and chewed her lip. 'Oh yes, of course, silly me! The thing is, can you give this to your dad? I mean, I would but I thought if you did, then it might not look like I was – well, you know, being pushy.' She thrust a padded envelope at Emma, and wiped her nose with the back of her hand. 'Look, I must fly – I promised Mum I'd wash her hair for her. We've found this rather nice hair colour, sort of peachy blond it says on the packet and . . .'

'Lovely,' Emma said firmly. 'Look, I must go.'

'Sure, fine, yes. See you tomorrow. I'm having such fun here – your dad is such a nice man, thinking of me, and he did say to keep him in touch with things and I said, yes, I would and . . .'

And with that Emma grabbed her bag and flew out of the back door, leaving Lily still talking.

The moment Emma got back to her own bedroom, having chucked the envelope on her father's desk, installed Harriet in the guest room (and assured her that yes, the bathrobe was for her to wear and no, she hadn't broken the taps – they switched off on their own because her father was so waste-conscious), she flopped down on the bed, grabbed her laptop and ran her eye down the incoming messages until she found the one she had known for sure would be there.

To: EmmaWH@talktalk.net
From: Lucyinthesky@hotmail.com

Hi! So how's it going? Got your text about Harriet's boyfriend. I died laughing about the penguins: unreal! Everything's cool here; the chalet's OK, or at least it will be when I've finished with it. Apparently two guys had it last and you should have seen the bathroom – gross! Anyway, I've already been to the market and got throws and plants and loads of floor cushions to cover up the grotty carpet and it's looking really cool. Adam's chalet is next door but one – he's sharing with an Aussie guy but hopefully he'll spend most of the time with me! And guess what? Angus – he's the camp leader – has said I can help organise the weekly swimming gala and maybe teach diving – isn't that great?

Emma sighed and shook her head in disbelief. Some people's idea of cool was way off centre.

So what did George say about the party? It had better be a massive 'Yes' because Adam is so psyched up. I reckon he thinks this is his chance to prove to big brother that he's in a cool crowd too! But there's so much to sort – bands, food, decorations . . . Freddie talks big but, when it comes to detail, he's useless. We're relying on you, OK?

Don't forget it's my birthday Wednesday – and it's my day off! So how about you meet me for lunch? Mum's sent me a pretty decent cheque so I feel a big spend coming on.

Got to go – Adam's playing in the staff against the kids football match and I'm in charge of cheerleaders! There's a really fit guy here called Luke – not that I'm interested of course, but I'll try and fix it for you to meet him when you come over. Even you couldn't resist him!

Get back to me and dish the dirt on the county set! Hugs, Lucy

Why, Emma thought, clicking on the Reply button, did everyone think she needed a guy in order to be fulfilled? She had a life plan and the slot for a serious relationship wasn't scheduled for another five years, after she had got her degree and established herself in her own business. Then, and only then, would she think about getting serious with someone from the City with a view to marriage (on her terms, of course and with a pre-nup) at around twenty-eight. Till then, guys were fine for the occasional snog – Freddie for one – but beyond that, forget it.

To: Lucyinthesky@hotmail.com
From: EmmaWH@talktalk.net

Hi! Glad you've got your laptop – I ran out of space when I tried to text and there's so much to tell you! First of all, THE PARTY'S ON! The Knightleys are fine about it, so you can tell Freddie it's a goer. Wednesday's fine – I'll pick you up at 11 – and please get it into your head that I am NOT INTERESTED in guys, OK? Unless, of course, they are for someone else – I just have to tell you about my latest stroke of genius. Theo Elton – remember him? Well, he's staying with George for a bit and I just know he's perfect for Harriet. I mean, think about it: he's dead sensitive and she needs someone like that, what with her mother . . .

She paused, and then deleted the last four words. She reckoned Harriet didn't need the whole world to know about her mother.

and she needs a guy with money because she's totally skint. He's moderately fit and he's got style, unlike that loser, Rob. The whole thing's perfect. And before you say that I'm going off on one – get this. Tonight, Harriet was laying the breakfast tables for tomorrow and she asked George if it was OK for her to go to church in the morning. I know, I was pretty gobsmacked – like you'd go out of choice? I never had her down as a holy type. Anyway, George said no, sorry, but he couldn't spare her unless I took on her chores. Like that was going to happen. I had to think fast, I can tell you, but I said something about having to help Dad sort out stuff for the film crew and he swallowed that one. Anyway, just at that moment, Theo came in (he'd been to Brighton for the evening). Harriet was looking all mis and he asked what was wrong; she told him about the church thing and guess what? He goes striding off after George and, two minutes later, George is saying that it's fine, she can go because Theo's offered to cover her breakfast shift! Get that! He must fancy her – I mean, have you heard of a guy actually choosing to get up early on a Sunday? Of course, his dad's a vicar so maybe it's in his genes, but anyway . . .

A knock on her door interrupted her flow.

'Dad?'

'No, it's me – Harriet.'

'Hang on!'

Emma scanned the final paragraph of her email.

Got to go – more tomorrow. See you Wednesday. Hugs, Emma.

She clicked on *Send*, and shut off her laptop.

'OK, come in!' she called, glancing at her watch as Harriet came into the room. 'I thought you'd be asleep by now – you looked done in.'

'I am, only . . .' Harriet hesitated, chewing her bottom lip and sighing.

'What? Do you need something? More pillows?'

'No, everything's lovely,' Harriet assured her, perching on the end of Emma's bed. 'It's – well, it's Rob.'

'Oh.'

'See, I rang him a bit earlier and he sounded really cheesed off . . .'

'Probably jealous that you've got a job that doesn't involve crustaceans and screaming kids,' Emma commented, suddenly feeling too tired to be compassionate.

'No, it's because he says he's going to miss me,' Harriet went on, apparently oblivious to Emma's sarcasm. 'Anyway, he's just rung back and said sorry for being off – and guess what? He thinks he could get me a job at Sea Life because this girl Rachel in the coffee shop has handed in her notice.'

'No way!' Emma exploded. 'You don't mean to tell me that after all my efforts getting you a decent job with really cool people —'

'Well, no, I did say I couldn't let you all down at the moment but . . .'

'Good!'

'And that's when he asked me what was more

important: this job or us getting the chance to spend more time together.'

She sighed and looked imploringly at Emma.

'It's really hard – I mean, he's so cute and him saying that – well, it must mean he fancies me, right?'

'It means,' said Emma forcefully, 'that he's into emotional blackmail big time. Still, it's up to you, of course. If you want to throw away the opportunity of a lifetime, there's not much I can do about it.'

She eyed Harriet solemnly.

'Freddie's party is going to be *the* social event of the summer,' she insisted. 'And there's the village festival, Dad's TV show, Charity Race Day – I could organise it for us to get into the Members' enclosure if we agreed to sell raffle tickets.'

She was pleased to note that Harriet's mouth was dropping open by the second, so she went in for the final whammy.

'It's not like you get loads of opportunities to mix with high-flying types like the Churchill crowd. Did you tell Rob about that?'

'Yes, and he said that's all just about image and snobs and social climbers,' Harriet replied ingenuously.

'Am I a snob? Am I a social climber?' Emma demanded.

'No, of course not . . .'

'Right – and neither are my friends,' Emma stressed. 'It just goes to show that Rob hasn't got a clue about what really counts. Still, if you'd rather be with him than here with me . . .'

'Of course I wouldn't! I've had more fun this evening than I've had in the last five years!'

This, thought Emma, as she smiled kindly at her friend, was just another indication of what a sad little life Harriet Smith had led until now.

'And the hotel is just stunning,' Harriet babbled, going off at a tangent. 'Did you know that the rooms are all named after the families that have lived there since sixteen something? And those crests on the wall in the dining room – they were put there by Sir Casper Knightley who . . .'

'Harriet, I've been going to that house since I was in pre-prep,' Emma cut in wearily. 'There's nothing you can tell me that I don't know already. And if you think tonight was fun – well, I promise it'll get even better.' She paused and eyed Harriet sternly. 'Of course, if you did take the job at Sea Life – which I can't stop you doing, and I wouldn't even try if that's what you really want . . .'

'Thanks.'

'But if you did decide to throw away all this, you wouldn't be able to bum off to church at a moment's notice. There won't be a Theo around to fight your corner.'

'Theo's lovely, isn't he?' Harriet smiled. 'And you're right – he was so sweet, offering to do my shift.'

'Precisely,' Emma said nodding, relieved to have finally got her point across. 'When was the last time this Rob person put himself out for you? He didn't even turn up at the club. Come to think of it, he didn't even let you know he wasn't coming. And he put work before a party. Whereas Theo . . .' She let the words hang in the air just long enough for Harriet to colour up ever so slightly.

'Theo seems to be really interested in you,' she finished.

'Don't be silly! Theo . . . interested in . . . I mean, he only met me today.'

'Sexual chemistry,' Emma told her wisely, remembering Lucy's phrase. 'Trust me – he's keen.'

Harriet's eyes widened. 'You think so? Really? A guy like that?'

'I know so,' Emma assured her. 'Ask any of my friends – when it comes to reading guys, I am never wrong. Remember how he came right up close to you on the croquet lawn? And he said to me . . . well, never mind what he said to me.'

'He talked about me?'

'Oh yes,' Emma nodded. 'All he needs is just a little bit of encouragement . . . but, anyway, it's none of my business. If it's Rob you want, then it's Rob you must go after.' She frowned thoughtfully. 'Of course, I'm probably not being fair,' she said. 'Just because I'm not boy mad . . . maybe you and Rob are really soul mates. I mean, is he into music like you are?'

'No way.' Harriet giggled. 'Do you know, he didn't know the difference between Berlioz and Bizet! I wanted him to come with me to that amazing open air concert at Preston Abbey – it was free, so I could actually go —'

'Lovely,' murmured Emma, who actually preferred R & B to classical music. 'And what did he say?'

'He couldn't make it,' Harriet said. 'He has tank cleaning training that evening.'

'I rest my case,' Emma said calmly. 'Whereas Theo, who probably has a thousand better things to do tomorrow than serving breakfasts . . . still, as I said, it's up to you.' She yawned. 'Now if you don't mind, I'm crashing out. I'll leave you to decide what to do. Life is all about making the right choices.'

'So I'll tell Rob no, right?'

'Your choice. Night, Harriet. Sleep well.'

✗ CHAPTER 5 ✗

Secret scheme:
Spend of the plastic, worry later

'DAD! WHAT ON EARTH ARE YOU DOING?'

Emma, blasted awake at half past seven on Sunday morning by what sounded like dustbin lids being scraped along a brick wall, burst into her father's den, hair tousled and feeling seriously sleep deprived.

'Dad!' She punched the Off button on his vintage Bang and Olufsen. 'You woke me up!' she shouted accusingly.

Her father glanced at his solar-powered watch. 'It's not early,' he commented. 'I thought you'd be over the way helping out by now. Besides, I'm so buzzed by this band.' He gestured towards the deck. 'That package from Lily – it had this demo CD in it. Great band – they're called Split Bamboo and the lead guitarist is . . .'

'Jake Fairfax,' concluded Emma with a groan. 'Lily's oh-so-amazing cousin.' She eyed her father closely. 'You're not telling me this band of his is actually any good?'

'They're more than good, they're going places,' her

father declared. 'I've read a bit about them in the music papers. One of their songs – 'Panic Stations Planet' – is very of the moment . . .'

'So that's why you're keen – because they're waving the green flag,' teased Emma. 'Never mind the music, just listen to the message, is that it?'

'Wouldn't do you any harm to take note,' her father muttered, pulling open a drawer and waving a bunch of Emma's most recent shopping receipts in her face. 'Look at this lot – High Wire, Stella Stein, Rock On Robin! How can you pay one hundred and five pounds for a handbag? It's obscene.'

'It's not just a bag, Dad, it's a Valentine Rockport bag . . .'

'A bag's a bag,' he said emphatically. 'And I'll bet none of these clothes are Fair Trade. Do you realise they were probably made in some sweatshop in Bangladesh with —'

'Yeah, yeah, OK, I'm sorry,' Emma assured him. 'Anyway, Dad, listen – I've just sorted the Knightleys' problems. Surely that deserves being let off the hook?'

She told her father about the party, how she was the mover and shaker and how she reckoned to double the Donwell profits overnight.

'Excellent!' Her father gave her a hug. 'What an opportunity for them! Well done you!'

Emma glowed under his obvious approbation.

'We can LOAF it,' he said. 'I'll talk to this new chef and have a word with Mrs P and —'

'We can what?' Emma demanded suspiciously.

'Don't you ever listen to anything I say?' her father

asked. 'LOAF – Locally grown, Organic, Animal friendly and Fair Trade. Oh, I can see it now – we'll get the press round – the Churchill name will ensure that – and we'll have organic wines, locally produced food and flowers – no air miles there, you see – and I could —'

'Dad, stop it!' Emma shouted. 'What's with all this "we"?'

'George's mother phoned me – she's worried about everything here. Says that old Coles, the estate manager, is losing his grip and she's not sure George has enough experience to deal with everything. So I assured her that I'd keep a firm hand on the tiller till they get back. Now where do you think we could source —'

'Dad, let's get one thing clear, right? No way are you going to embarrass me by getting on your soapbox and going all moral. Besides, it's not as if one party is going to make a difference.'

'Emma, it's that attitude that is slowly crucifying our planet,' her father insisted. 'I shall speak to George.'

'Don't you dare!' Emma snapped. 'You wanted me to have a job, right? Well, I've got one.' She kissed the top of his head, always the first step towards wrapping him around her little finger.

'Yes, and I'm pleased,' he began.

'So just let me get on with it, OK?' she pleaded. 'You just concentrate on the TV show.'

'Good grief!' her father exclaimed, jumping up. 'I'm supposed to be having a video conferencing call with the production director at half past eight. Thank goodness you reminded me.' He flicked off a few switches and headed for the door. 'Oh, and tell George that I've told our garden boys to go over and help out next door whenever he needs them,' he added.

'OK, and Dad?'

'Yes?'

'Can I have my August allowance?'

'Emma, it's the third of July,' her father pointed out. 'And the answer is no.'

Oh well, thought Emma, thank heavens for Visa.

'Hi Emma! How are you doing? I'm just making pancakes – those little American kids were asking for them.'

Lily didn't pause in her batter-beating as Emma peered round the door of the hotel kitchen, but just kept on talking.

'I know they're not on the menu, but like I said to Luigi, it's no trouble for me, cos I love to cook and this is such fun and, anyway, we ought to cater for everyone's needs and Americans do like their pancakes, and they're checking out today so it's the last chance, only there isn't any maple syrup so I said let's try them with honey —'

'Where's Theo?' Emma butted in. She knew from years of experience that the only way to deal with Lily's babble was to ignore it.

'Theo? Oh, he's just driving Harriet to church.'

'*Driving* her?' Emma gasped. 'It's only ten minutes' walk!'

'Oh no, she's not going to St Margaret's – some of the guests had an early breakfast to get to the service there – but no, Harriet said St Benedict's, and of course that's quite a way.'

'And so Theo took her?' Emma exploded. 'That is so

{ 76 }

not on – he's supposed to be waiting at tables.'

She checked herself, her mind racing. Miffed as she was at the thought that she might have to step in and work, it must mean that Theo actually wanted the chance to get to know Harriet a bit better. She'd known they were made for one another the moment she had seen them together on the lawn, but she was pretty chuffed at the speed of his response.

'OK, pancakes done!' Lily said triumphantly, sliding the last one on to a plate. 'They're for table five.'

'And you expect me to . . .?' Emma began, looked around the room. There was nothing for it; she was the only one there. She picked up the plate.

'A gem, this Lily, she is a gem!' Luigi appeared from the walk in pantry and beamed at Lily. 'I tell her, when she is qualified, I give her a job.' He sniffed and glanced around the kitchen. 'Though not here – here I don't stay for long. That Mrs P – she drive me crazy. I deserve greater things than this.'

'Don't tell the Colonel that,' Emma cut in with a smile. 'He was eulogising over your crème brûlée last night.'

'He was? Is true I have a gift . . . perhaps tonight I give him my flambéed peaches with the raspberry coulis?'

'That would be wonderful!' Emma declared. As she pushed open the door to the dining room, she noted that Luigi's face positively glowed with delight. Human Relations – that was what life was all about, she told herself, deftly stepping to one side to avoid tripping over Phoebe Pilkington's Barbie caravan. There was nothing that couldn't be achieved by simply reading people and boosting their egos.

After she had pacified the American kids for the absence of maple syrup by assuring them that Superman always ate his pancakes with honey, and besides, this was special honey as eaten on the film set of *Harry Potter and the Order of the Phoenix*, she returned to the kitchen to find the back door open and Theo spooning coffee into a cafetière.

'Hi! One worshipper safely delivered,' he announced. 'I said I'd pick her up about one o'clock.'

'That's a pretty long church service,' Emma exclaimed.

Theo laughed. 'She's going to have coffee with her mother afterwards,' he told her. 'At the hospital. St B's is the hospital church. That's why she wanted to go there.'

'She told you?' Emma was staggered. 'About her mum?'

'Oh yes,' he said nodding. 'She told me everything. Pretty tough life she's had, poor girl. And you know I was thinking, if I asked her —'

'Omelettes, table one,' Luigi shouted, slamming two plates on to the serving trolley. 'Bagels, table three.'

'Please,' said Emma sweetly, gesturing to Theo to take the plates.

'Me?' He looked at her aghast.

'You were doing Harriet's job, right?' Emma reminded him. 'Well, this is it.'

'Oh. Yes. Right. Fine.' He picked up the plates somewhat gingerly. 'Don't disappear, though,' he said. 'I need to tell you about this stunning idea Harriet had.'

Stunning and Harriet in the same sentence? It's a start, thought Emma. And whatever the idea, all I have to do is agree with it.

* * *

'You know the old photographs of Donwell in days gone by?' Theo said half an hour later as he and Emma stood at the conservatory door, watching as George explained the finer points of archery to half a dozen enthusiastic wrinklies. 'The ones on the staircase?'

'Mmm,' Emma murmured through a mouthful of left-over scrambled egg.

'Well, Harriet reckoned we should put them on the website beside up-to-date photographs of the same places.'

'Wow!' Emma was momentarily taken aback. Harriet clearly had more about her than she'd thought. 'You mean,' she ventured eagerly, 'like that sepia photo of the orangery in 1880 superimposed with guys working out at the health club that's there now? And maybe, that one of the boating party on the lake before the First World War merged in with one of people fishing for trout there now?'

Theo's eyes widened. 'Gosh, I hadn't thought of it like that, with people doing stuff,' he enthused. 'You're amazing.'

'It was Harriet's idea,' Emma pointed out.

'Well, yes, but she never said it like that,' he gabbled. 'Hey, why don't we try it out, right? We could make a start now with you playing tennis on the court by the orchard – the one where Vita Sackville-West had her picture taken.'

'Theo, I hate to remind you, but tennis is a game for two and if you're taking the photos . . .'

'Oh that's OK,' Theo assured her. 'You just hit a few balls over the net and I'll click away. So – can you get changed?'

'Why not wait till Harriet gets back?' Emma suggested. 'You could use her – after all, it was her idea.'

'No way,' Theo said hastily. 'See, the thing is, she said she wasn't terribly sporty and I'd hate to embarrass her. Like you said, she's a bit self-conscious. I could tell that talking to her in the car.'

'OK, I'll give it my best shot,' Emma agreed, chuffed at his obvious concern for Harriet's feelings.

'Oh very good!' Theo laughed. 'Best shot? Tennis? Nice one!'

It was a start, Emma thought as she held up each of her three tennis outfits in turn. She'd read that worrying about a girl's feelings was a sure sign of a burgeoning love interest. Now it was up to her to do all in her power to make it burgeon very quickly.

'Make it look like you're serving an ace,' Theo ordered, adjusting his telephoto lens. 'And again! Nice one. And . . . hang on, where are you going?'

They had only been on the courts for five minutes when Emma threw her racquet on to the ground as the strains of 'Funky Foot Rock' rang out from her mobile phone deadening the birdsong from the nearby beech trees.

One new message!

She shaded her eyes from the sun and scanned the screen.

Ring me! Now! Lucy x.

Emma speed dialled Lucy's number. 'Lucy, it's me. What's up?'

'Sorry about the text – running out of credit. Look, I'll have to talk fast because I've got to teach water polo in ten minutes,' Lucy gabbled. 'But you know it's my birthday on Wednesday, right? Well, I'm ringing to invite you to The Jacaranda Tree.'

'You can't,' Emma replied. 'I mean, nice idea – but you have to be a member.'

'Or be invited by a member,' Lucy retaliated smugly. 'Freddie's one. Or rather, he belongs to some swish club in London that has reciprocals.'

'Freddie? He's down here already?' Emma gasped. This was serious: her roots were showing and she hadn't had a French manicure in ten days.

'Emma! Hurry up!' Theo shouted from the other side of the court. 'We're wasting time.'

Like this is time wasted, she thought.

'He's not coming till Wednesday – he's meeting us at The J Tree at eight,' Lucy said. 'Apparently, there's this band headlining there – he heard them when they played at the May Ball at Cambridge. He says they are totally ace, and he might try to get them for the party.'

'This band,' Emma queried tentatively. 'What's it called?'

'Oh, I can't remember,' Lucy said with a sigh. 'Broken Stick – no, that's not it.'

'Split Bamboo,' Emma suggested.

'That's it!' exclaimed Lucy. 'Have you heard of them?'

'Oh yes, loads,' Emma replied. She paused, her mind working overtime. If Freddie really wanted this band, and she could make it seem like she was the only person on earth who could make it happen . . . 'But unfortunately, they're in huge demand and I doubt he'd have an ice cube's chance in hell of getting them,' she said. 'But then, on the other hand, if I could have a word with Dad and get him to pull a few strings . . .'

'Would you? Could you?' Lucy burst out. 'See, Adam's so desperate for everything to go right. He and Freddie – well, they drifted apart a bit, what with living different lives and stuff – and now it looks like they could be really good mates.'

'Let me see what I can do,' Emma said sweetly. 'So come on, what's the plan for Wednesday? Who's invited? Oh my God, what am I going to wear?'

If she hadn't been so clued up about other people's emotions, Emma would have been tempted to think that Theo was given to sulking. The moment she had got off the line to Lucy she had gone in search of her father, Theo trailing after her, camera in hand, moaning about losing the light and putting his schedule totally out of sync.

'I've got to go and get Harriet in a couple of hours,' he muttered. 'I wanted to take a whole lot of pictures before then.'

Bless, thought Emma. He's not moody, he's just desperate to impress her.

'Shouldn't you put the ones you've already got on to the website before you fetch Harriet?' she suggested, suddenly inspired. 'After all, she's bound to want to see them, and we don't know they're going to work.'

'Oh sure, they'll work,' Theo said airily. 'It's a doddle, that kind of stuff.'

'Yes but – well, it *is* my picture and I'd feel better knowing it looked OK. I might need you to do some digital enhancement.'

Theo laughed. 'Hardly,' he said. 'But if it'll make you feel better, I'll do it now. Don't worry, I'll catch up with you later.'

You are such a negotiator, Emma told herself proudly, as Theo headed off towards the main house. She was just turning towards her father's office when Lily Bates came running up the drive.

'Emma! Emma, wait!'

There was no avoiding her, so Emma fixed a smile on her face and waited.

'Isn't it exciting? Oh my God, Jake is like so over the moon! Isn't your dad a star?'

'Lily, what are you on about?'

'Your dad – TV Today – I mean, never in a million years did we think —'

'LILY!' Emma shouted. 'Slow down. What about TV Today?'

'They're coming to film your dad's programme.'

'Well, I know that, silly.'

'And your dad said how would it be if he could work it so that Jake's band got a . . . oh, silly me, what did he call it? You know, one of these fly-on-the-wall things, when it seems like a coincidence that they're around, only it's not really because he's set it up?'

'He said that?'

'Yes, really!' Lily nodded. 'See, your dad called in on Mum to get Jake's phone number and, of course, Mum said no need, he's here and then —'

'Jake is at your place? Now?'

'Sure, and your dad's giving him loads of contacts for bookings and —'

'*What?* Oh my God – come on, let's go!'

'Where?'

'To your place. I simply have to meet Jake. Now.'

Jake Fairfax looked more like a nineteenth-century Romantic poet than an upcoming rock star. He was tall and skinny, with a pale face that tapered into a dimpled chin and eyes of such icy blue that they seemed almost transparent. His unruly mop of corn-coloured hair looked as if it had been attached to his head as an afterthought by a rather second-rate doll-maker and his fingers constantly fiddled with the blue and white scarf knotted round his neck despite the temperature being well into the twenties. What's more, neither his bum nor his lips (the two areas of a guy that Emma always checked out first) were of the sort to appeal to her: his backside was too flat and his lips too full. He looked about sixteen. But there was something about him that fascinated her. For one thing, when he smiled, his eyes stayed sad-looking, which could of course be due to the grief of losing his girlfriend; and, for another, his voice was totally out of keeping with his body. It was deep and husky and of the sort that, had she heard it without seeing him, would most definitely have turned her on.

'If you're looking for your dad, he's just left, dear,' Mrs Bates said, manoeuvring her wheelchair into the corner of the room and gesturing to Emma to sit down. 'Did Lily tell you about the wonderful news?'

'Yes, I heard everything,' Emma said quickly. 'Jake, it's so cool you being here because we need you up at Donwell to play at a party.'

'We don't do private parties,' Jake said amiably. 'We're concentrating on penetrating the club scene.'

'Have one of these,' Lily butted in, thrusting a plate under Emma's nose. 'Mini brioche – I had to do them at college for my exam and I got excellent for them, but these are better still because I used —'

'This isn't just any party,' Emma countered briskly, taking a pastry just to shut Lily up and wondering whether this Jake guy wasn't just a little bit up his own backside. 'It's Freddie Churchill's twenty-first! You know, the guy in the Carstairs adverts?'

Emma was rewarded to see Jake's face flush and his eyes widen.

'Freddie Churchill? He's having a party down here?'

'Uh-huh, and he heard you play at Cambridge and was totally blown away,' Emma went on. 'So much so that he's taking a whole crowd of us to hear you at The Jacaranda Tree. On Wednesday.'

'On Wednesday? Freddie Churchill is coming to the club?' Jake's eyes widened in disbelief.

'You know him?' Lily cut in. 'You never said.'

'I don't know him, exactly,' Jake replied hastily. '*Tatler* were taking his picture at the May Ball and I asked someone who he was and we had a quick chat. That's all.'

'Is he as gorgeous as he looks on the adverts?' Lily asked. 'I drool at the one where he takes off his shirt and dives into the waterfall.'

'I didn't really take much notice,' Jake said with a shrug. 'Mind you, he seemed to be pretty popular with the girls.'

'So anyway, will you do it?' Emma urged, dusting crumbs off her shorts. 'July twenty-third at Donwell Abbey. He'll pay well.'

'Like I said, we don't do parties,' Jake repeated. 'But – well, maybe if he wants to talk about it on Wednesday when the rest of the guys are there, we'll see.'

He stood up and flexed his shoulders. 'Got to go, Auntie,' he said, smiling at Mrs Bates and planting a kiss on the top of her head. 'Sitting here won't find us somewhere to stay.' He paused, his hand on the doorknob. 'Say, why don't you come to The J Tree as well? You've never heard us play live.'

'That's sweet of you, dear,' his aunt replied, 'but to be honest, it's not my sort of scene and I get so tired by the evening. But Lily would love to go, wouldn't you, poppet? And you don't work on Wednesday nights.'

'Wow, yes that would be great!'

Mrs Bates turned to Emma. 'You'd give her a lift, wouldn't you?'

'Well, I would, but it's Lucy's birthday and we'll probably be going on to another club or —' She stopped as she saw Jake eyeing her closely. '. . . But I'm sure that'll be fine,' she finished. Falling out with Jake at this point was not a good idea and, if enduring Lily for one evening meant getting Split Bamboo for the party, it was a small price to pay.

'Bless you, dear,' Mrs Bates went on. 'Poor Lily – she doesn't have much fun with me like this.'

'Mum, just stop that,' Lily ordered. 'We have a great time. And I'm not going anywhere till I've found someone to come and sit with you. And I'll leave a nice salad and a glass of wine, and we'll get you ready for bed before I go and —'

It struck Emma that Lily's life really wasn't a bundle of laughs.

'I'll ask my dad to pop in and see you too,' Emma said on impulse. She wasn't sure her dad would be around, but at least making the offer made her feel better.

'I do hope the boys find somewhere nice to stay,' Mrs Bates said as Jake left. 'They can't afford much and there's four of them. I don't like the idea of some grubby hostel.'

Suddenly, everything clicked into place in Emma's brain.

'Mrs Bates,' she murmured, smiling her most endearing smile and patting her hand the way she'd seen them do on *Holby City* and *ER*, 'don't you worry. I think I have the perfect solution. Just leave it with me.'

'Emma, you're a star!'

'That is just the coolest idea!'

Adam and Lucy sat side-by-side on the steps of Lucy's chalet later that afternoon and gazed up at her admiringly.

'See why I had to come over and tell you to your face? Neat, isn't it?' Emma agreed, squatting down beside them. 'Dad's chuffed because the band is staying in the eco-lodges – that way he gets them into the show without it looking contrived – Jake's over the moon because Dad's waiving the rent and I reckon now there is no way the band can refuse to play at Freddie's party. So come on – where do we go to celebrate?'

'Nowhere, sadly.' Adam sighed. 'We're both on duty this evening – I'm teaching raft-building for tomorrow's raft race, and Lucy's helping with the campfire sing-along.'

'Ye gods, you two lead riveting lives!' Emma teased, gazing round at the groups of kids playing rounders or clambering over the assault course. 'All looks like pretty hard work to me.'

'Not half as hard as some of the lives these kids lead,' Adam replied solemnly. 'I've got a boy in my football squad who looks after his blind mum and dad – and he's only nine. A charity paid for him to come and it's the first time he's had a chance to be a kid.'

'A bit like Lily,' Emma murmured thoughtfully. 'You don't realise, do you? I mean, what with our lives and stuff.'

'No,' Lucy replied. 'You don't.'

For a moment, the silence was broken only by the shrieks of delight from the kids on the bouncy castle.

'So how is your other scheme going?' Lucy said smiling, anxious to lighten the mood. 'You're not really serious about getting Theo and Harriet together, are you?'

'Theo? Theo Elton?' Adam butted in. 'He's with Verity Price – although don't ask me what he sees in her. She's a right little tart.'

'Which is why he's not with her now,' Emma informed him, deciding not to mention that it was Verity who chucked Theo. 'And why Harriet is so perfect for him.'

Her mind went back to the way Harriet had chatted non-stop when she got back to Emma's house earlier that afternoon.

'Theo was just so lovely with Mum,' Harriet had told her, kicking off her shoes and sinking down on to one of the rattan chairs on the terrace. 'He chatted away —'

'You mean, you took him to meet her?'

'When he came to fetch me,' Harriet had explained. 'He insisted on going and saying hi. Mum doesn't normally like strangers coming, but she really took to Theo.'

'More than Rob?' Emma had asked, working hard to keep her voice disinterested and neutral.

'Oh, Rob's never been to the hospital,' Harriet had replied, glancing at her watch. 'I haven't said much about Mum's illness to him.'

'But you felt able to tell Theo, who you only met yesterday?' Emma had murmured. 'That's interesting.'

'Well, yes – I mean, no – I mean, I will tell Rob, of course, it's just that I didn't want to put him off.'

'I can see that.' Emma had nodded wisely, as her mobile phone bleeped. 'Obviously, if you're aware that Rob's that shallow —'

'I didn't say that,' Harriet had interrupted hastily. 'He's just not really keen on hospitals.'

'But if he was keen on you . . . oh, don't listen to me.' Emma had said theatrically, pulling her phone from the back pocket of her jeans and noting with some satisfaction how Harriet's expression changed to one of confusion.

She had scanned the text message.

Have you got Harriet's mobile number? Theo x

She hadn't been able to restrain a gasp of delight.

'There, I told you Theo was keen – if you don't believe

me, look at that!' she had cried, thrusting the phone under Harriet's nose. 'Shall I send it to him?'

Harriet had nodded so rapidly that she resembled a plastic dog in the back of a Robin Reliant.

'Wow! I mean, do you really think he likes me?'

Emma giggled as she remembered Harriet's joyful expression. She rammed her sunglasses on top of her head and turned to Lucy and Adam.

'So I did,' she told them, having left out the bit of the story involving psychiatric hospitals and divided loyalties. 'And then I came over here and left them to it.'

'Bring them along on Wednesday,' Lucy suggested with a grin. 'Then I can see whether all this is just a figment of your imagination.'

'OK, cool.' Emma nodded standing up and brushing bits of grass from her shorts. 'Oh well, I suppose – good grief, what's that noise?'

She winced as the screech of a siren sent a flock of starlings flying from the trees.

'The klaxon for supper,' Lucy told her. 'Got to dash. I'm on sausage duty.'

'The way some people choose to spend their summer defies belief,' sighed Emma. 'I'm going home to wax my legs and watch *Fifteen Love* . . . See ya!'

❦ CHAPTER 6 ❧

Daring dream:
Pull the A-list guy and make sure everyone's looking

'GUESS WHAT?' HARRIET CRIED, BURSTING FROM THE sitting room on Monday morning as Emma was waving goodbye to the last of the weekend guests. 'George has just said I can play the piano – you know, the baby grand in the back sitting room? It's fantastic – we had to sell ours. Well, no, that's not true. They came and took it away because Dad didn't keep up the payments.'

Too much information, thought Emma. She'd have to teach Harriet that, while honesty was great in theory, there were times when it was best kept under wraps.

'Lovely,' she said. 'By the way, that was such a cool idea of yours – about the photos on the website.'

'Oh, that.' Harriet smiled. 'It wasn't my idea – I saw it on Mum's hospital website. You know, nurses in starched caps pushing old-fashioned bath chairs alongside modern-day therapists, that kind of stuff.'

'Well, anyway,' Emma persisted. 'Theo's thrilled. By the way, did he phone you after I texted your number?'

Harriet nodded. 'He wanted me to help choose which

of your tennis pictures to put on the website.' She giggled. 'They're really ace . . . oh ha, ha! Ace? Tennis?'

Even their sense of humour matches, thought Emma and then winced at her own choice of words.

'I told him to put music on the website,' Harriet went on. 'You know, the right period for each picture. He's asked me to sort it for him.'

'Brilliant!' Emma had to confess that Harriet was a constant source of amazement. She looked so dippy and yet she had some great ideas, which of course was exactly what a guy like Theo needed.

'The pictures of me were just practice shots,' she said. 'It's you he wants to photograph. He said you were really pretty.'

'He did? Really?'

'Mmm,' Emma murmured. 'Which is lovely, considering.'

'Considering what? That I'm not really pretty, you mean? Well, I know —'

'No, silly. Considering he's so desperately in need of someone to love him.'

Harriet's eyes widened. 'Theo is? But he's so fit – surely he's got a girlfriend?'

Emma composed her features into what she hoped was an expression of muted compassion. 'Had,' she whispered. 'Treated him brutally. Awful. Can't say more but he just needs to know people care.' She glanced at her watch. 'Gosh – is that the time? Must dash. So – if he asks for help with photos and stuff – well, you will sort of . . .'

'Of course I'll help. Poor guy – and he's so lovely.'

Emma left feeling that the day had got off to an exceptionally good start.

'Look, Theo, much as I'd love you to keep taking pictures of me, I simply can't let them go on the website,' Emma was saying to Theo ten minutes later after he'd cornered her in the hallway and asked her to pose in the rose garden. 'My father would go ballistic.' She paused, wondering how to make her excuse sound convincing. 'See, Dad says he doesn't want my name associated with anything that's not one hundred per cent environmentally OK. You know, what with him being high profile and stuff. He loves the Knightleys to bits but the hotel isn't exactly eco aware and —'

'Right.' Theo nodded. 'I can see his point. But it was such a good idea of Harriet's.'

'So use her,' Emma went on. 'It might help to boost her self-esteem. And she's free all day.'

'You are kind,' he said. 'I'll do that then.'

'Oh and by the way, Lucy's invited you and Harriet to The Jacaranda Tree on Wednesday. You up for it?'

'You bet!' he replied. 'Hey, I could take some shots for the teen bit of the website. That would spice it up a bit! From Croquet to the Club Scene – great caption, eh?'

'Brilliant.' Emma smiled. 'See you.'

At ten o'clock on Tuesday morning, Emma was sitting at her dressing table plucking her eyebrows when her phone rang.

'Emma? Where the hell are you?'

She held the phone away from her left ear and

continued plucking with her other hand. 'In my bedroom. Not that it's any business of yours,' she informed George.

'Actually, business is exactly what it is. Mrs Paxton-Whyte is here with Annabelle,' he hissed. 'Wedding plans? You said you'd take on Mum's role and Mum is never late!'

Emma chucked the tweezers to one side and kicked herself for looking inefficient in front of George. 'OK, tell them I've been on the phone to some rather upmarket florists.'

'Have you?'

'No, of course I haven't, but they don't know that. George just do it, OK? I'll be there in ten minutes.'

An hour later, having resisted the urge to burst out laughing at the thought of the robustly built Annabelle Paxton-Whyte dressed as Titania for her *Midsummer Night's Dream* wedding ('My fiancé is going to be Oberon and my bridesmaids will be fairies – isn't that blissful?'), Emma was hurrying down the drive to pick up her car and go into Brighton for some serious retail therapy. (The excuse she'd given to George was the need for gossamer-like tulle in sugar pink for the tables, but the main attraction was Gear Up's sale.) As she reached the gates, a white Porsche 911 shot round the corner from the lane narrowly missing clipping her on the toes.

'You bloody idiot!' she screamed, leaping back on to the grass as the car shot past and then screeched to a halt, its tyres spinning on the gravel. 'What the hell do you think you're doing?' Emma's heart was racing as she bent down to try to wrest the heel of her slingback from the soft turf and promptly toppled over. 'You could have killed me!'

'I am so sorry!' A shadow fell across her face as the guy jumped out of the car and came towards her. 'Let me help.'

'Bit late for that!' she muttered 'What kind of loser —?'

She looked up and her mouth fell open. The thick, blond hair and grey-green eyes of the guy smiling wryly down at her were instantly recognisable. It was Freddie Churchill.

'What are you doing here? You're not meant to be coming till tomorrow.'

Freddie laughed and reached out a hand to pull her to her feet. He was wearing steel grey Fendi cut-offs and a baggy T-shirt; his arms and legs had the natural tan of someone who, when he wasn't sailing or rowing on the Cam, was lounging about at some friend's villa; and his whole air was one of confident self-assurance that comes from knowing that, even if you fluff all your exams, someone somewhere will bail you out.

'I've always thought plans were made to be altered,' he said, flashing her a smile. 'Besides it's your fault.'

Emma brushed grass clippings off her dress and tried to look sophisticated.

'How do you make that out?' she said, wishing she hadn't sucked off all her lip gloss and had done something with her so-in-need-of-highlights hair.

'Adam says that you think this Donwell Abbey place is an OK venue for my bash,' he said shrugging. 'So I thought I'd come and suss it out.' He grinned at her.

'Come on, why don't you show me round? I mean, unless you're going somewhere?'

'Nowhere that won't keep, I guess,' Emma said, trying not to sound too enthusiastic. So – what do you want to see first?'

'And we could have champagne on the terrace to start, then move to the dining room and conservatory for food and then the band and disco can be in the marquee,' Emma concluded twenty minutes later. 'Assuming, of course, that Jake says yes.'

'Jake? You've spoken to Jake? You mean – the guitarist with Split Bamboo?'

'Sure I have,' Emma said sweetly. 'He's the cousin of a dear friend of mine.'

'And you sorted it?'

'Well, not every last detail,' she admitted. 'He's insisting on speaking to you on Wednesday. But it should be fine. Now, is there anything else you want to know?'

'Yes, just one thing,' Freddie said, moving closer to her. 'Will you do it?'

'Do what?' Emma's heart missed a beat.

'Be my party planner,' he pleaded. 'I love parties, I just hate all the aggro that goes into organising them.'

For a moment, Emma couldn't speak. She was too busy running a preview of press cuttings in her imagination:

Churchill party a stunner thanks to Emma Woodhouse.

Celebs clamour to retain services of Brighton's hippest party planner.

'Sorry, I shouldn't have asked,' Freddie said apologetically. 'I'll get someone else . . .'

'No, no, I'd love to do it!' Emma enthused. 'Now, about the fireworks . . .'

'I did it, I did it, I did it!'

Emma burst into the sitting room where George was picking ticks out of Brodie's matted coat.

'Did what?'

'Only secured you the most high-profile booking Donwell has ever had,' she raved. 'Freddie was here – he's ever so nice and he's booked every room from Thursday night through to Monday morning. He thinks my idea of a fancy dress theme for the party is ace, and he wants fireworks and the marquee on the lawn for the dancing and everything!'

George jumped to his feet, ignoring Brodie's yelp as he trod on his paw. 'You mean, it's actually going ahead?' he gasped.

'Uh-huh,' Emma replied. 'It's so cool – he's having a couple of dozen really close mates to stay and the rest will just come for the party. Loads of people from the fashion business, so you never know where that might lead.'

'So where is the guy?'

'He's gone,' Emma told him.

'And he left a deposit?'

'What?'

'Emma you didn't let him go without – for heaven's sake!' George exploded.

'I couldn't ask him for money,' Emma reasoned. 'He's Adam's half-brother. And he's really nice.'

'Oh, and what are you going to say when he doesn't pay the party bill? *Oh George, it's OK, he's really nice.* Get real, Emma!'

Emma glared at him. 'You know what, George Knightley? You're becoming a real bore. He gave me his card, I gave him my phone number. And if you're so worried, ask him for the money yourself!' she snapped.

'You said he'd gone.'

'He has, but you'll see him tomorrow at The Jacaranda. Lucy's party? She said she'd left a message on your answerphone.'

'Yes but —'

'And don't start all that "I'm needed here" bit,' Emma ranted. 'There aren't any guests right now. Dad's around. And besides, call it work. Checking out the Churchill credit rating.'

To her relief, George's face creased into a smile. 'OK, OK. I'm sorry – it's just that all this is such a responsibility.'

'So let your hair down for once,' Emma encouraged him. 'Come and listen to the band and . . . oh sugar!'

'Now what?'

'I forgot to tell Freddie that Split Bamboo were staying over at our place.' She sighed. 'They're moving in tonight. Still, maybe it's best – Jake is still being all precious about playing at the party. Hopefully Freddie will persuade him. He's ever so nice.'

'If you say that one more time,' muttered George, 'I might just decide to hate the guy on sight.'

'I can't believe Freddie's down here and hasn't been in

touch,' said Lucy for the fifth time on Wednesday as she and Emma, exhausted from three hours' hard shopping, sat in Fitzherbert's eating *salade niçoise* and sipping cranberry juice spritzers. 'Adam'll be gutted. Did he say he'd come over later?'

Emma shook her head. 'He got a phone call from someone called Judy while we were talking and he dashed off,' she reported. 'He seemed in a bit of a state, to be honest.'

'Judy?' Lucy frowned, fingering the moonstone bracelet that was Emma's birthday gift to her. 'Girlfriend, maybe?'

'Has he got one?' Emma replied, a little too quickly.

'I guess he must have,' Lucy mused. 'Guys like that with loads of money and a body to die for – he's hardly going to be sitting at home watching Corrie every night, is he?' She eyed Emma. 'Not that you'd care, anyway,' she teased. 'You're not into guys.'

True, thought Emma, sipping her drink. But just think what a coup it would be to pull Freddie Churchill in front of everyone, especially if he's supposedly at the beck and call of this Judy girl. In that instant, she doubled her resolve that, when Freddie hosted his birthday bash, it would be her and no one else that would be at his side.

The Jacaranda Tree was the latest addition to the Brighton club scene. Three floors, all lavender and pink perspex with chrome pillars and huge screens picking out the bands and dancers, were already filling up when Emma, George, Lily, Harriet and Theo arrived on

Wednesday evening. One mention of the Churchill name and they were waved past the bouncers and down the stairs. Emma caught sight of Adam and Lucy, perched on stools by the bar that encircled the giant purple plastic and vinyl tree which stretched from the basement to the roof of the building and gave the club its name.

'Now this is the business,' Theo declared, whipping out his digital camera and fiddling with the setting. 'Better than a picture of some old bloke!'

'Where's this Freddie guy, then?' George demanded as Theo began clicking away.

'So Emma, what can I get you to drink?' Emma retorted, pushing her way closer to the bar. 'Thank you, George. Since you're driving, I'll have a Sassy Surfer please.'

'OK, OK.' George sighed, pulling out his wallet. 'Lily, what about you?'

'Oh, wow,' Lily exclaimed. 'Um, well, maybe an orange juice – no, no, this is a special night, isn't it, so perhaps a Bacardi and Coke? I haven't had one of those since Christmas. But, then again, it made me go all silly . . .'

'Sillier than usual?' Emma muttered to Theo under her breath.

'. . . so perhaps a vodka tonic? I mean, with your dad looking after Mum, I could I guess have a drink and . . . well, I've never had vodka but Melanie – she's on my catering course – she drinks it all the time and she's really sophisticated, so —'

'LILY!' Emma snapped. 'Bacardi or vodka? Which?'

'Um – vodka. Please. Thanks.'

'And Harriet?' George eyed his wallet cautiously.

'I'll get the rest!' Theo butted in, turning to Harriet. 'Just make sure you choose some flash-looking cocktail then I can capture you on film for the website!'

As they reached the bar, Emma saw that Adam was on his mobile and he didn't look happy.

'It's Freddie,' Lucy hissed at her. 'He's still not here and the band are due to start in ten minutes. And his phone's switched off.'

'You don't think he's with this Judy girl?' Emma asked, anxiously.

'So what if he is? He can bring a whole bloody harem as long as he gets here. Adam's been psyching himself all day.'

He's not the only one, thought Emma.

'He's not coming.' Adam's face was scarlet as he shoved his mobile phone into Lucy's hand. 'Go on read it – see if you can make sense of it.'

Lucy peered at the screen.

Major crisis. Can't make it 2nite. Be sure u get band sorted 4 me. C u l8r. F

'What does he mean, "crisis"?' Adam demanded. 'It was his idea to come here. So much for all his "don't worry about the cost, I'll pay".'

'So this is your "ever so nice guy", is it?' George muttered in Emma's ear, as cheers broke out around the club at the appearance on stage of Split Bamboo. 'I bet the next thing will be that he bottles out of the party booking.'

'He won't,' Emma snapped, cross that all her plans had to go on hold. 'The poor guy's in the middle of a crisis and all you can do is slag him off!'

'I didn't . . .'

Emma didn't stay to listen to George's feeble attempts at self-justification, but followed Adam and Lucy who were pushing their way through the throng to the edge of the stage where the band was already into the opening bars of their signature hit, 'Lift off Love'.

'Is Adam really gutted?' she whispered to Lucy. 'Because if it's the money, I'll pay for the next lot of drinks and —'

'That's so sweet of you,' Lucy said, giving her a hug. 'But it's fine; we'll hear the band and then go on to Mango's or some place where the drinks aren't the price of an all-over body massage!'

'Come on, babes, come and dance,' Adam said, slipping an arm round Lucy's shoulder and kissing her. 'To hell with Freddie – let's party!'

'What *is* Theo doing with that wretched camera?'

George had finally got over his bad mood and was moving – Emma didn't think his gyrations warranted being called dancing – to the final Split Bamboo hit when they were almost blinded by the camera flash.

'Taking pictures of Harriet,' Emma said, gesturing behind her to where Harriet was leaning on the bar talking to Lily. 'He's clearly falling in love with her.'

'Falling in – Emma, what are you on?' George asked as the band struck their final chord and announced a break. 'Theo and Harriet? Get real!'

'And what's so odd about that?' Emma demanded. 'They're made for one another. He's on the rebound.'

'Oh right, and that's a real basis for a new

relationship,' George replied, taking Emma's arm and heading for the bar. 'Besides, when he does get it together with someone else, it won't be a Harriet, that's for sure.'

'What's wrong with her?'

'Nothing – she's a nice girl, in a ditsy kind of way,' George said, shrugging. 'But no way is Harriet going to tick any of Theo's boxes.'

'Oh and Verity the Tart did?'

'Absolutely. He only went for Verity because her father's a senior consultant at the Royal Free. Theo's a friend, but I know him and he's a snob and he's very ambitious.'

'And you are such a bad judge of character,' Emma declared.

'Emma, if Theo's keen on anyone, it's you, not Harriet,' George muttered.

'Me? Oh please – he hangs round Harriet all time. Just you wait – I give it another few days and those two will be lip-to-lip twenty-four seven. I know the chemistry.'

'Really?' George laughed. 'So how come you haven't used all these amazing skills to find yourself a guy? Or have you?'

'My skills have been employed in fighting them off,' Emma retorted. 'When I do meet a guy who's got what it takes, I'll give it all I've got.'

'And you haven't come across him yet?'

'Not even on the distant horizon. Now, are you going to get me another drink, or do I have to die of dehydration?'

* * *

'Aren't they amazing?' Lily gripped Emma's arm as the band drifted off to a quiet corner. 'I love them all. Of course, Jake's the best – isn't his voice great? The drummer with dark hair, that's Ravi; and Nick's on bass and the guy with the saxophone, he's . . .'

'Dylan,' Emma finished for her.

'You know them?'

'Lily, their names are on their T-shirts,' Emma pointed out.

'Oh yes. Silly me. Wow, that drink's gone straight to my knees. Anyway, this girl came up to me and she said she thought the band would be real chart-toppers and I said I was Jake's cousin and she asked me for my autograph!'

'My goodness, someone on the planet sillier than you,' Emma murmured.

'Sorry, what did you say? It's so noisy in here.'

'I said, why don't you come with me and persuade Jake to play for the party?' Emma said, smiling brightly.

'Sure, yes, oh right – oh, hang on!'

Emma turned to see a tall girl wearing an electric blue sundress and far too much lip gloss waving a postcard in Lily's face. 'I didn't want your autograph, dimbo – I wanted you to get the guys' autographs. Didn't you hear me? Are you deaf as well as dumb?'

'Oh, silly me. He's over there – why don't you . . .?'

'We'll get it for you,' Emma cut in, grabbing the postcard in one hand and Lily's arm with the other and dragging her over to the band.

'Hi, Jake! You were stunning. I mean, out of this world amazing,' Emma began.

'Thanks.'

'Freddie's in pieces not to be here,' Emma rattled on. 'Work crisis – that's what comes of being a mega star.'

'Really.' Jake didn't seem impressed.

'But he wanted me to sort the arrangements for the party. I mean, I know you said you didn't do parties but . . .'

'But you will, won't you?' Lily burst in. 'I mean, Emma's my best friend and her dad has been so good to Mum – he's with her right now, they're going to watch a programme about the Lake District because she went before she got ill and . . .'

'So what time do you want us there?' Jake asked with a wry smile.

Emma gasped. 'So you'll do it?'

'Yeah, the guys are up for it,' he said. 'But I'll need to talk to Freddie face to face to get the low-down on what he's looking for. No offence, but that's the way we operate.'

'Sure.' Emma shrugged. 'He'll be around all week, I guess.'

'Good,' said Jake. 'When you see him, tell him to give me a call. Pronto.' He scribbled on a card and tossed it at Emma.

'Oh, and some girl wanted your autographs,' Emma said hastily, shoving the postcard under his nose.

Jake laughed. 'Some girl, eh? I wouldn't have thought you were the shy and bashful type.'

'It's not me!' Emma exclaimed. 'As if . . .'

But Jake had already turned away to talk to another wide-eyed fan.

'Hey, do you think he fancies you?' Lily gushed. 'Hey, wouldn't that be —'

'Lily?'

'Yes?'

'Shut up.'

'I can't believe it's not even a week since I was sitting here and you told me about the job,' Harriet said an hour later when everyone had moved on to Mango Monkey's. 'I was telling Rob about —'

'Rob? You've seen Rob?'

Harriet shook her head. 'He sent me a text,' she explained. 'Look!'

She pulled her mobile from the clutch bag that Emma had been on the point of giving to the charity shop before Harriet had taken a liking to it. 'Read it. It's sweet.'

Reluctantly, Emma took the phone and began scrolling through the message.

Hi! Gr8 news. They've put me on C Turtles! And upped the £. Cool, eh? When r u coming over? Xx

Emma didn't deign to make a comment. She simply looked at Harriet and raised an eyebrow.

'He wants to see me,' Harriet enthused. 'And he put two kisses and guys don't do that if they're not keen and I put two as well when I texted him back.'

'Harriet, guys who are keen don't talk about turtles,' she said, in a knowing voice. 'And as for asking you over . . .' She paused as Harriet's phone beeped in her hand. 'Don't tell me this is him again,' she muttered, chucking the phone at Harriet. 'What is it this time? A run-down of the life cycle of the stingray?'

Harriet didn't reply. She was staring at the phone

open-mouthed. Emma peered over her shoulder.

I'm outside, you're inside. Not a good plan. Come and meet me by the fountain. Theo xxx

'Yes, yes, yes!' Emma punched the air and hugged Harriet. 'Now *that's* a romantic message. Go on, then!'

'But – I didn't realise he was – I mean, you think he really likes me?'

'What have I been telling you all week?' Emma remarked smugly. 'Now go on – go and find out just how much he likes you.'

She watched as Harriet hurried through the press of dancers towards the door. Then she picked up her drink and went to share her moment of triumph with George.

'So come on, tell me everything! Did he kiss you?' Emma urged the instant that George had dropped them off at the front door of her house.

'No,' Harriet replied, 'but he was really sweet. At first he seemed surprised that I'd gone out there. I guess he thought I'd go all precious on him . . .'

'And?'

'Well, he kept looking over his shoulder like he was scared someone would see us, but then he took my hand . . .'

'Promising,' murmured Emma, slipping her key into the lock. 'Go on.'

'And he showed me all the stars and told me their names. And then he asked me to go and dance and we did. Well, for a moment or two. He asked how my mum was getting on, and then he said he'd better go and chat to you because you were all on your own. That was kind, wasn't it? Oh, and before he went, he said he'd drive me over to see Mum some time this week.'

This, thought Emma with satisfaction, is definitely love.

Harriet let out a dreamy sigh. 'Rob never . . .' She hesitated.

'Never had a romantic bone in his body? Never noticed the stars?' Emma urged.

Harriet bit her lip and said nothing, and Emma wondered for a second if she was being a bit too harsh.

'Rob's busy, of course,' Harriet finally said, 'and really hard working and stuff, which is why he can't . . . but yes, Theo's lovely, but so's Rob and . . . oh, I don't know.'

'Well, look at it this way,' Emma said cheerfully. 'If you hang out with Theo for a bit, and make Rob jealous, he might be more attentive. You've nothing to lose.'

Harriet sighed again. 'You're right. And you know, Theo is terribly sweet. And I do like him a lot.' She smiled at Emma. 'In fact, it was just the best evening ever.'

✄ CHAPTER 7 ✄

Secret scheme:
Somehow find a way out of this one

FOR THE NEXT WEEK, EMMA WAS IN HER ELEMENT. EVERY day provided yet another opportunity to put her people-sorting skills to good use.

On Friday the problem was Freddie's continued absence.

'His mobile's off all the time,' Lucy said on the phone to Emma that morning. 'Adam called in at the gallery in case his grandmother knew anything.'

'And?'

Lucy sighed. 'All she would say is that Freddie had left a note to say he'd be away for a bit. No reason why. Adam was really miffed, especially when his gran said that Freddie was a grown man and could take care of himself. She's totally off this planet.'

'She does have a point, I guess,' Emma acknowledged.

'Yeah, but you know what Adam thinks? He reckons that Freddie's father's calling the shots again, and Freddie's gone home, which means no party here, which means —'

'Lucy, get a grip!' Emma ordered. 'Leave it with me, OK? I'll sort it.'

'Oh, like you're really going to make him switch his phone back on? How? By telepathic communication?'

'No, Luce, by using my brain. I'll call you later. Bye!'

'*Country Matters* photographic department, Bianca Richards speaking. How may I help you?'

'I'm so sorry to bother you,' Emma replied. 'I'm trying to find Freddie Churchill. I understand he's doing photo shoots for you about now.'

'I'm afraid I am not allowed to release details of —'

'Of course not. It's just that I'm the functions manager of Donwell Abbey and he asked me to be sure to call him today but the number he gave me isn't being recognised. I wonder if you can tell me where I might find him?'

'Hold the line a moment please.'

Emma tapped her foot impatiently and sent up a silent prayer.

'We can't give out his details, but I could contact him for you at the hospital and —'

'Hospital? Is he ill?' Emma's heart missed a beat.

'No, he's fine, and forget I said that, OK?' There was a note of panic in the girl's voice. 'I'm only here on work experience, and they'd kill me . . .'

'I've already forgotten,' Emma said with as much charm as she could muster. 'If you can get him to phone me, I very much doubt that I will remember.'

'And your name?'

'Emma Woodhouse. Tell him that it's about the band. Oh, and his brother.'

No harm in setting a few hares running in a good cause, she thought.

'Will do. And thanks.'

It was, thought Emma, chucking her phone to one side, very satisfying to have people eating out of your hand.

'Emma? Freddie here. 'Look, I'm calling from the hospital.'

'What's happened?'

'Er, oh, well this mate of mine messed up big time in a pub the other night,' he said. 'Took E – landed up in hospital and —'

'That's awful! Was it, I mean, it wasn't this Judy person, was it? The one who phoned you?'

'Ju— well, yes, actually it was,' Freddie said. 'I'm sure someone spiked the drink or something. I mean, no matter what, no one would take that stuff out of choice, surely?'

For a moment, he sounded like he was about to burst into tears.

'Look, I can't talk here – hospital rules,' he went on hastily. 'The girl at the office said something about Adam? Is he OK?'

'Worried sick about you. But all right, if that's what you mean,' Emma replied briskly.

'Right, thank God for that. Can't do with any more crises. And actually, I'd rather you didn't say too much about what I've just told you – it's hardly the kind of thing you want the world to know about.'

'I guess not. What shall I tell Adam?'

'Oh, just say something about work overload – I'll be down in a few days anyway.'

'Great. And about the party – what shall I . . .?'

'The band's the main thing – and as you've got them —'

'You knew? Who told you?'

Freddie laughed. 'You said you would sort it and, according to Adam, you always get your own way, so I just assumed,' he explained hastily. 'Don't tell me they said no?'

'Of course not,' Emma replied. 'As if they'd dare. What's more, I wangled it so that they're staying at our place. Cool or what?'

'That's brilliant. Oh look, I've got to go,' Freddie said hurriedly. 'Oh, and Emma?'

'Yes?'

'Thanks. You're a star. I owe you one.'

Great, thought Emma. That's one debt I'll be collecting very soon.

'Ecstasy?' Lucy gasped after Emma had rushed over to the Frontier Adventure Centre in her car. 'The girl must be a raving lunatic to mess with that stuff.'

'I get the feeling Freddie was pretty disgusted with her,' Emma replied. 'It's odd though.'

'How do you mean?'

'Well, I've been thinking. Judy phoned Freddie in the middle of the day when he was with me and she must have been fine then.'

'And?'

'Well, he dashed straight off, right? So surely he'd have been with her that evening. And if he was, how come he didn't stop her taking it? Doesn't make sense.'

{112}

'Perhaps they had a row,' said Lucy. 'Perhaps he was working. And why are you so bothered?'

'I'm not,' Emma protested. 'And listen, he doesn't want anyone to know. Adam's to think it was work.'

'I don't keep any secrets from Adam,' Lucy said at once. 'But I'll tell him to keep quiet about it.' She looked thoughtful. 'I hope this Judy doesn't make a habit of taking drugs. If she does, he needs to get out of there quick,' she muttered.

'Well,' Emma said, winking at her. 'We'll just have to make sure that he finds someone with far more savvy to hang out with, won't we?'

'Emma? Are you saying what I think you're saying?'

'Me? I'm not saying anything. But watch this space!'

Max Knightley had been discharged from hospital, and he and Sara would be home in a couple of days. George's father was still in some pain, but the doctors felt that the stress of not knowing what was going on in his beloved home was slowing his recovery.

'So you see,' Emma told Luigi, whispering confidentially in order to boost his ego, 'you can't leave now. Not after George has sent so many emails to his parents saying how amazing your food is.'

'He did?'

'And of course, Mr Knightley is going to need to build up his strength and, to be honest, stodgy food is so not the thing. We really need you, Luigi – *he* really needs you.'

'I stay. I make him my special minestrone and perhaps my tagliatelle verde and —'

'Whatever,' Emma said hastily. 'Must dash. Things to do. *Ciao*, Luigi!

On Monday, the crew from TV Today arrived in Ditchdean, an event that had the whole village in a state of heightened excitement, and Harriet and Lily positively hyperventilating. Emma was pretty fired up too, but in her case it had little to do with the possibility of ten seconds of screen time.

She had been in the conservatory at Donwell measuring up for netting to hold the hundred odd balloons she'd ordered on Freddie's behalf, when she overheard something that stopped her dead in her tracks.

'I've met this amazing girl.'

Theo was standing outside on the terrace, his phone pressed to his ear.

'Verity? Oh, forget Verity – she's history!' she heard him exclaim.

Emma edged closer thankful for the vast parlour palm in its bronze urn that screened her from view.

'Anyway, you'll get to meet her because I'm going to ask her to the Regatta Ball. And I thought we could join your table, yes?'

Emma had to stifle the desire to punch the air in triumph. Another challenge – to get Harriet fit for *the* social event of the Brighton Marina year. She guessed her friend didn't know the first thing about sailing, not that ignorance had ever stopped Emma having a great time. All you had to do was drop in a few references to spinnakers and yawing and mainsails, and you were home and dry. But of course, she mused, Harriet doesn't have my social skills so I'm going to have to get to work fast.

'OK, see you there then! Great. Bye, Mum!'

Emma did a double take. This was his mother he was talking to! Which, depending how you looked at it, was great news or the worst thing in the world. Great, because if Theo was already at the 'meet the parents' stage, things were progressing even better than Emma could have hoped; and worst thing because Theo was hardly likely to snog Harriet senseless in front of his parents, particularly as one was a canon in the Church of England and the other a JP whose frequent letters to the Editor of the *Evening Argus* were for the most part scathing condemnations of what she called 'the lack of personal boundaries in society today'.

She slipped quietly out of the conservatory, ran across the hall and out of the door, eager to find Harriet and prime her before Theo got to her.

'Emma, darling – just the person we need!' Her father came hurrying across the lawn towards her, clipboard in hand. 'I've got to take Sean – he's the producer – and the crew round the village so they can sort locations for the opening shots. We're doing all the pre-recorded stuff this week ready for the live show later, you see.'

'Fine, but what's that got to do with me?'

'I want to get the band into some of the shots,' he said, dropping his voice as the producer came within earshot. 'So I thought if you could get them to set up on the lawn, make it look like they're rehearsing for a gig when we get back, then I can talk about the eco-message behind their music and they'll see how it fits in with the theme of the show.'

'You know what, Dad? Sometimes you're quite on the ball!' Emma teased. 'OK I'll sort it. By the way have you seen Harriet?'

'She's over in one of the lodges, getting autographs from the guys.' Tarquin laughed. 'She'll do you good, you know, Emma.'

'Her do me good? How do you work that one out?'

'She's very ecologically minded,' her father explained. 'She knew all about sheep's fleece insulation and photovoltaic panels.'

'They'll make good chat-up lines, then, won't they?' Emma replied.

'What? You think Harriet's keen on one of the guys in the band?' her father asked.

She'd better not be, thought Emma. Not now that Theo is about to get his act together and declare undying love. But just in case . . .

'Got to dash, Dad. See you!'

'So – now do you believe me? I mean, what guy takes a girl to the Regatta Ball if he's not keen?'

Emma smiled smugly at Harriet who had reverted back to her 'surprised goldfish' expression.

'I don't believe it!' Harriet gasped. 'I mean, are you sure?'

'Of course I'm sure,' Emma said, laughing. 'I heard it with my own ears. Now, it's not long till the ball so we need to go shopping for something sexy enough to turn

Theo on, but subtle enough to keep the parents happy. Then your hair. I thought —'

'Hang on,' Harriet said, smiling. 'If you're right, and Theo really does like me – well, he likes me as I am. There's no need to go overboard.'

'Harriet,' Emma replied as calmly as she could. 'When it comes to guys, you should leave nothing to chance. Trust me, I know.'

It was late on Tuesday morning when Emma, bursting into the office at Donwell, saw the final proof that her scheme had worked.

Harriet was sitting in front of the computer, and Theo was standing at her side, his arm resting lightly on the back of the chair. On the screen was a whole collage of photographs. And Harriet was in every one.

'That's stunning,' Emma exclaimed, as Theo clicked on the mouse and ran through the pages of the website. Each set of photographs were accompanied by music – chamber music, *Music for the Royal Fireworks*, 'In an English Country Garden' – all suited to the individual photos. 'Those club shots are brilliant! Getting one of George looking relaxed was a triumph!'

'We're just choosing which ones of Harriet I should print off and get framed,' Theo explained.

'Great idea,' Emma said, over the moon at such a romantic gesture. 'Adam's grandmother has some really great frames down at the gallery. Why don't you —?'

She was interrupted by an impatient shrilling of the reception desk bell.

'What now?' she muttered. Since George was at the

airport meeting his parents and Lily was doing something creative in the kitchen for the TV crew's lunch, Emma reluctantly stuck her head around the office door.

Standing impatiently, tapping his fingers on the desk and looking distinctly harassed, was Freddie Churchill.

'Oh good, it's you,' he said, grinning. 'I need to talk to you. It's about the band.'

He paused and stepped back as the office door opened and Theo emerged, followed by a very excited looking Harriet.

'We're going out,' Theo announced.

'But I'll be back in time for the TV people's suppers, I promise,' Harriet added.

'Has he asked you about the ball?' Emma silently mouthed the words at Harriet, who shook her head. Clearly, she thought, this was going to be the moment. He'd ask her on the way to the gallery. She winked at her friend.

'Have fun,' she said. 'Oh, and by the way, this is Freddie. Freddie, this is Theo Elton, and that's Harriet.'

Theo glanced at him, said a brief 'Hi there,' and turned to Harriet who had turned bright pink.

'So are you coming or not? I haven't got all day,' Theo demanded, cutting into her stammered greeting.

OK, so his delivery could do with a little refining, thought Emma, but he's clearly just desperate to get her on her own.

'Sorry,' Harriet said meekly.

Emma turned to Freddie who was fingering the pile of *What's On in Sussex* leaflets on the desk. 'What was it you wanted? And have you told Adam you're around?'

Freddie laughed. 'Sure, I phoned him,' he said. 'He was in the middle of five aside football. Not best pleased —'

'He'd have been even less pleased if you'd done a runner again,' Emma assured him. 'What can I do for you?'

'I've only got about an hour – we're doing a photo shoot at Beachy Head later,' he said. 'Apparently the windswept look is in!' He took a deep breath. 'But I wondered if any of the guys from the band were around? You said they were staying here.'

'Not here,' Emma corrected him. 'Next door at my place. Come on, I'll take you over. Always assuming they're not too caught up in their moment of fame and glory.'

'What?'

Emma explained about *Going Green* and her father's determination to get Split Bamboo on screen.

'And they're filming now? Shit! That's all I need. When does the show go out?'

Emma frowned. 'Not for ages. They've got the programme proper to do yet. Anyway, what's the problem?'

'What? Oh, no problem. I'm just pushed for time and if they're busy —'

'Doesn't look like it!' Emma laughed as they reached the top of the Hartfield drive and saw the four guys lying on their backs, bare-chested, sunning themselves on the lawn.

'Hi guys!' she called. 'Number One Fan approaching!'

Ravi and Jake propped themselves up on their elbows and squinted in the bright sunlight.

'Freddie?' Jake sprang to his feet. 'This is great!' He paused. 'I mean, it is Freddie Churchill, right?' he queried, glancing at Emma. 'Thought I recognised you.'

'Yes, it's me,' Freddie replied. 'Look, can we go somewhere and sort stuff out?'

'Sure,' Jake said. 'Come over to the lodge.' He turned to the others. 'You guys don't need to come. Just be ready if the TV crew return and give me a shout, yeah?'

'I'll leave you to it, then,' Emma said reluctantly. 'But we need time, too, Freddie – there's still loads of things to sort out.'

'No probs,' Freddie said, 'I'll give you a call. *Ciao!*'

And with that he and Jake disappeared towards the lodge.

The Knightleys arrived back at Donwell late on Tuesday afternoon. Mrs Knightley, looking stunning as usual in white trousers and a cerise silk kaftan, admitted that they had timed their arrival to coincide with the quiet part of the week, and was a little perturbed to find the *TV Today* people milling about. Certainly Max's pale face and slightly laboured breathing suggested that the last thing he needed was to be forced to make cheerful small talk; while George's mother was desperate to catch up on everything that had been going on since they left, all her husband wanted was to sit in the conservatory with his beloved dogs and a large whisky. It wasn't until she had made sure that he was comfortable and had quietly removed the bottle of Glenmorangie to a safe hiding place, that she sank down at the kitchen table beside George and gratefully took the mug of tea that Emma had made for her.

'I just don't know what we would have done without you two,' she said, smiling wearily at them. 'You're a star, Emma, to rally round.'

'It wasn't just me,' Emma admitted. 'Harriet, and Lily —'

'Oh yes, and Theo.' Sara nodded. 'Well, I've been thinking. I'm afraid we're going to need all the help we can get for a bit longer. This nasty business has really taken the wind out of Max's sails.' For a moment, her eyes filled with tears, and George leaned over and squeezed her hand. 'It's this big party that worries me,' his mother continued. 'I know it's just what we need, but all that planning . . .'

'Don't you give it a thought,' Emma told her. 'It's all under control. Luigi and Mrs P have actually stopped arguing and decided to share the menu – he's doing canapés and something very inventive with wild duck and venison, and Mrs P is making a meringue pyramid and every recipe out of her *Sussex Puddings Through the Ages* book!'

Mrs Knightley looked relieved. 'And you'll deal with everything?'

'Of course,' Emma assured her. 'Hey, you know what? I reckon you and Max need a bit of down time on your own, right?'

'Well, it would be —'

'So how about tomorrow night, we all clear off and leave you in peace?'

'Emma,' George protested. 'There's the TV crew to deal with.'

'That's where you're wrong,' she said. 'Dad told me just now that they reckon they'll have all the shots in the bag by tomorrow evening and they're all eating out at some place the producer likes in Kemp Town. Which means we're free to . . . which means your mum and dad can have peace and quiet.'

'That would be lovely,' George's mother admitted. 'Besides, you all deserve to have a bit of fun after your hard work.'

'Brilliant! I'll tell Freddie,' Emma announced.

'What's he got to do with it?' George muttered.

'He texted me,' Emma said. 'He's got this great idea – Split Bamboo have got a warm-up slot tomorrow night for Shellshocked's Gig on the Beach, right? So we're all going there early on.'

'All?'

'Adam, Lucy, Theo and Harriet, I guess, me, you . . .'

'Count me out,' George said. 'I've heard the band once and they're not that amazing.'

'Oh George, don't be such a party pooper,' Emma pleaded. 'Loads of the gang from Deepdale Hall will be there.'

'And that's meant to be an incentive?' George said, joking.

'After the gig, Freddie wants to do the silly scene – you know, slot machines on the pier, helter-skelter, ice-cream sundaes,' Emma enthused. 'It'll be a laugh. Go on.'

'Well, if you insist.' George grinned.

'I do,' Emma retorted with a smile. 'I'll even buy you candy floss.'

'So where's Theo? Did he ask you?' Emma pounced on Harriet when she returned to Hartfield later that afternoon.

'No,' Harriet said. 'He came and saw Mum with me for a bit.'

'You went to see your *mother*?' Emma exclaimed. As romantic venues went, she put this on a par with shopping at Tesco.

'Yes, and then he left – said he had to go shopping – and he picked me up later, and we came home. But he did talk about the ball.'

'And?' Emma pressed her eagerly.

'He said when it was on, and he said he was a hopeless dancer.'

'That's true!'

'And then he said, did I think a girl would mind going to a ball with someone who had two left feet? And I said, of course they wouldn't mind but then . . .'

'What?'

'Then he stopped talking about it.'

'Oh. You shouldn't have let him.'

'I had no choice. He shut up because he got stopped for speeding.'

The whole stretch of beach between Brighton's Palace Pier and the stark silhouette of the burned-out remnants of the West Pier was heaving with people by the time the gang finally got there. Theo had refused to drive, glaring at his car as though it was to blame for his speeding ticket and no one else wanted to miss out on the cocktails, so they'd piled into a couple of taxis and spent half an hour in a traffic jam.

'Freddie's here somewhere,' Adam said, scanning the crowds. 'He came early – said he'd save us a space near the band.'

'Like he's going to be able to do that,' muttered George.

'There he is!' Lucy cried, pointing to the long stone breakwater stretching into the sea.

Freddie was standing on the breakwater, waving both arms in the air to attract their attention and gesturing wildly that they should join him.

'If that's Freddie Churchill,' said George, 'then he's a total idiot.'

His words had no effect on Adam and Lucy as they headed off to the promenade end of the seaweed-strewn breakwater and began scrambling on to the top, closely followed by Harriet and Lily, the latter giggling like a school kid. Emma spotted Serena and Chelsea hovering nearby, gazing up at Freddie.

'There's no way they'll be allowed to stay up there,' Theo said. 'They'll get sent off before the band's even started.' He turned to Emma. 'Why don't we go over to the Seaview Hotel, go up to the roof garden, buy a drink and watch it all from there?'

Emma shook her head. 'We've got passes to the stage side and, besides, the roof garden will be full of private parties,' she said, slightly perturbed that he wasn't rushing after Harriet, who had already lost a sandal on the shingle below and was scrabbling along the breakwater in a most uncoordinated manner. 'Very exclusive – bit like the Regatta Ball, I guess.' No harm getting his mind back on track, she thought.

He swung round and looked at her, his eyebrows knitting together in a frown. 'Are you going to that?' he stammered.

'No, but it's meant to be a really good night, and there's loads on, I mean – casino, silent auction – you don't have to even be a good dancer and —'

'AARGH!'

Even above the noise of the gathering crowd, Harriet's shriek could be clearly heard.

'Oh my God, she's fallen!' Emma screamed and began belting across the shingle as fast as her wedges would allow.

'Now are you satisfied, Freddie Churchill?' George muttered, hurrying after her. 'Harriet! Are you OK?'

It was clear, even before the words were out, that Harriet was far from OK. Her face was deathly white, and beads of perspiration were breaking out on her forehead. 'My ankle,' she moaned, tears beginning to trickle down her cheeks.

'Theo, go and get the St John Ambulance guys,' George ordered. 'Emma, go to the ice-cream van and ask for ice – and lots of it!'

He squatted down on the pebbles beside Harriet and took her hand. 'It's OK,' he said gently, 'just take deep breaths.'

'Theo's the medical student, not you,' Emma reminded him. 'He's the one who needs to be taking care of her.'

'I think I'm going to be sick,' Harriet whispered, and promptly was. Which, Emma reflected, did absolutely nothing for her distressed heroine image.

'Does anyone want to come with her in the ambulance?' the paramedic asked, raising his voice to be heard over the loudspeakers blaring out Split Bamboo's first number.

'Emma?' Harriet's voice was faint but pleading.

This is so not my scene, Emma thought. She had many strengths, she knew that, but hospitals she couldn't handle. She'd even felt her heart race at the sound of the ambulance's siren, never mind riding in the thing and risking Harriet puking again.

'Emma? Go on,' George urged.

'Theo, you go,' she pleaded.

'Me?' Theo queried. 'But surely you're her friend and —'

'I can't face it,' she said. 'Please.'

'Sure I'll go,' he said, squeezing her hand, and Emma realised that this was what he'd wanted all along. 'Now don't worry – she's going to be fine. And the hospital's only a couple of blocks away. I'll be back before you know it.'

As the ambulance pulled away and the small huddle of interested spectators turned their attention back to the stage in the middle of the beach, George pulled Emma to one side. 'If Freddie's thinking of playing the fool like this at his party, he can think again,' he said. 'I'm beginning to wish I'd never agreed to it. Mum would go ballistic if anything happened.'

'George, it'll be fine,' Emma assured him. 'It was just

bad luck, that's all. Besides, it's all my fault.'

'How do you make that out?' George asked.

'I didn't explain to them that we could just push through and go to the seats by the stage. Those passes that Dad gave us . . .'

She faltered, an image of Harriet's ashen face floating before her eyes.

'If I'd said something to Adam, he'd have told Freddie, and Freddie would never have climbed —'

'Freddie seems like the sort of daredevil idiot who'd do anything to attract attention,' said George. 'Poor Harriet. Well, thank God it wasn't you. And clearly Freddie's not bothered.' He gestured towards Freddie, who was clapping his hands over his head as the band played 'Panic Stations Planet'.

'He probably doesn't realise what happened,' Emma suggested, noting with some irritation that it was Chelsea Middleton Hyde in her minuscule denim shorts and slinky top to whom he was paying a considerable amount of attention.

'Oh, like he didn't spot the ambulance,' George retorted sarcastically. 'He realises all right. He just doesn't care.'

On way back. Where r u? Theo

Relief flooded through Emma's body as she read the text message. Harriet must be OK. The ambulance guys said it might only be a sprain. Now she could relax and start enjoying herself. All the fooling about on the pier, riding the Ghost Train and sliding down the helter-skelter had been no real fun with the thought of Harriet in the back of her mind all the time. Not to mention the rather uncomfortable sensation of guilt that she should have been with her, rather than stuffing herself on a Double Toffee Banoffee Sundae.

On way 2 Funky Seagull 2 dance r pants off! C U!

It wasn't until she had zapped the Send button that she realised that Harriet, however slight her injury, would be in no mood for dancing.

Never mind. She could watch, and Emma resolved to make a real fuss of her in between proving that she had what it took to pull Freddie. If only to wind George up.

Funky Seagull, a tiny club underneath the arches at Marine Drive, was packed. Emma had never been there before; Freddie had heard about it from one of the fashion shoot photographers and urged everyone to give it a go. Chelsea and Tabitha, who had somehow managed to attach themselves to the group, were already in the middle of the dance floor. The lighting was so dim that Emma could hardly make out where anyone was, but she did spot Ravi chatting up Lily – there was, she thought, no accounting for taste – and saw that Dylan and Nick were busy downing shots at the bar. Adam and Lucy were, as usual, locked in one another's arms, and Jake was nowhere to be seen.

So she had Freddie all to herself.

He was just beginning to respond to Emma's carefully honed chat-up lines when Theo tapped her on the shoulder.

'Theo!' she exclaimed. 'Where's Harriet?' She peered through the darkness in hopes of catching sight of her friend.

'At the hospital, of course.'

'You haven't left her there on her own?' Emma asked.

'Give us a break,' Theo protested. 'We'd been there ages and they said she'd be at least another hour.'

'So?'

'I said I wanted to get back to you and she said she'd be fine.'

'Well, of course she said that,' Emma shouted, raising her voice over the thumping of the music. 'It doesn't mean she meant it.'

This was serious. Theo was not acting like a guy in the grips of rampant desire.

'Women,' Freddie added dryly, 'always talk in opposites. And I should know.'

He grinned at them both, and, to Emma's annoyance, drifted back towards the bar.

'This isn't how I meant the evening to turn out,' Theo said a trifle forlornly. 'I had it all planned.'

'What did you have planned?' Emma asked hopefully.

'This.' He grabbed her, pulled her towards him and kissed her full on the lips.

'Oh Emma, if you knew how long I've wanted to do . . .'

The force of Emma's slap cut him off in mid sentence.

'What the hell do you think you're doing?' she gasped, pushing him away and trying to ignore Chelsea's thinly veiled smirk. 'Your girlfriend is lying injured in hospital and you have the nerve —'

'Girlfriend? The only girlfriend I want is you.' Theo held a hand to his cheek and stared at her in horror.

'But Harriet . . .'

'Harriet? Get real. You really think I'd waste my time on Harriet? Darling, you don't have to be jealous.'

'Don't you dare call me darling, you creep! Just get away from me.'

'How can you be like this?' Theo demanded, snatching her hand. 'You know you like me.'

'You arrogant, self-opinionated . . . as if!'

'Come off it – you practically fell over yourself to tell me you'd get me an invite to Freddie's party.'

'I was just being kind; it didn't mean anything. You were around and —'

'Why do you think I agreed to help George out in the first place? Like I didn't have better things to do. It was only because he said you were going to be working there and after that night at the South Downs Ball when you made it clear I was in with a chance . . .'

'What are you on? You're mad.'

'It was the first thing you mentioned when you saw me, so don't pretend it hadn't been on your mind too.'

'Nothing, but nothing, was further from my thoughts.'

'For God's sake, you led me on enough . . .'

'How dare you! I did no such thing – why would I? When it was Harriet who I wanted you . . .'

Emma was conscious of George, Jake and Lily turning in astonishment at the sound of her raised voice.

'*You* wanted? You mean to tell me that you were trying to get me and Harriet – it's ludicrous! Whatever made you think —'

'You took her to church, you even offered to do her shift.'

'Only so that I could do it with you,' he protested.

'You went in the ambulance.'

'I did that for you,' he snapped. 'Because you looked as white as a sheet at the thought of it.'

Emma swallowed hard. 'Well, what about the photos – you printed them and framed them, you sucked up to her mother, you told people that she was an amazing girl,' Emma spluttered.

'Oh, and when am I supposed to have done that?' he demanded.

'I heard you on the phone to your mother, talking about inviting her to the Regatta Ball.'

'Not her, *you!*' he shouted. 'It's you I want.'

For a moment Emma was speechless. Theo wasn't.

'As for the photos, she wanted me to print them off for her mother. And as for visiting the old bat, sure I did. My summer holiday assignment from med school is *"The Effects of Mental Illness on the Wider Family Unit"* – I wanted to see how Harriet interacted with her mother.'

'You know what? You are the pits,' Emma hissed. 'And what about that text at the club? Luring her outside and showing her the stars.'

By now Adam and Lucy had disentangled themselves from one another and were staring at her open-mouthed. Chelsea was edging closer to them, clearly desperate to catch their every word.

For the first time, Theo looked a little shamefaced. 'That text was meant for you,' he admitted, dropping his voice. 'I pressed the wrong name entry – Harriet's next to you on my address book.'

'But you danced with her, you spent time with her – she thought . . .'

'You said to be nice to her, so I was,' he said. 'I danced with her because I felt guilty about the text. In fact, I acted pretty damn well.'

'If that's acting well, I'd hate to be around when you acted badly,' Emma stormed. She shook her head and sighed.

'Please, can we just forget all this and start over?' Theo pleaded, pulling her towards him again.

'No, we can't!' she shouted, wriggling out of his grasp. 'You don't realise, do you? You have just wrecked Harriet's life.'

'What's going on?' George appeared at their side, a wide-eyed Lily right behind him.

'As of now, nothing. Theo was just leaving.'

'You know what you are, Emma?' Theo shouted. 'You're nothing but a scheming little —'

'Theo!' George burst out. 'Calm down, mate. What's all this about?'

'Ask her!' Theo spat, glaring at Emma.

'Look, why don't we —?' Adam cut in.

'Oh go to hell! Get lost, the bloody lot of you!' With that, Theo turned on his heel, and shoved his way to the door.

'I can't believe it,' Emma said tearfully to Lucy in the Ladies five minutes later. 'How could Theo imagine for even a second that I could be interested in him?'

'I don't know why you're surprised,' Lucy replied. 'Harriet's sweet but she's not Theo's type. Whereas you are. Looks, money, contacts . . .'

'That's just what George said.' Emma sighed. 'Why am I so dumb, Lucy?'

'You're not dumb,' Lucy said loyally. 'You just – well, you like arranging other people's lives. And remember, you got it right with Adam and me.'

'Well, I'm never going to try it again,' Emma pronounced, blotting her lip gloss and picking up her bag. 'But what am I going to say to Harriet? She was over the moon at the thought of the Regatta Ball.'

'The what?'

'Nothing.' Emma pushed open the door and walked back into the dimness of the club. 'Just another sign of my total uselessness.'

George was hovering near the door.

'Where's Freddie?' Emma asked.

'He's taken Jake home,' George said. 'He was feeling rough and since that lot . . .' He jerked his head towards the bar where Nick, Dylan and Ravi were play-punching one another and downing yet more drinks. '. . . are incapable of driving, Freddie said he'd run him home.' He eyed Emma closely. 'Anyway, what is it to you where he is?'

'Nothing.' Emma was miffed but, in all honesty, the fun had gone out of the evening and the last thing she felt like was flirting. 'I just need to call the hospital to find out what's happening to Harriet.'

'I already did,' George said. 'She's being discharged. It was just a bad sprain, nothing broken.'

'I've got to get home and be with her,' Emma said. 'Can you help me find a cab?'

'I'll come with you,' George said. 'I've had enough of this place anyway.' He took Emma's hand and began pushing his way through the crowd of dancers. 'Don't

{133}

worry,' he said gently. 'I know it's been a disastrous evening, but it's only a sprain and Harriet will be fine in a couple of days.'

Emma shook her head. 'Her foot may be,' she murmured. 'But it's her heart I'm worried about.'

As the taxi turned into the lane that led to Hartfield, Emma was relieved to see the light twinkling from the window of the guest bedroom.

'She's back,' she said. 'Oh George, what am I going to say to her? I should have listened to you – I got Theo all wrong.'

She expected a lecture from George but, instead, he was staring out of the taxi window.

'That's Freddie's car,' he said, gesturing to the Porsche parked in a lay-by near the bus stop. 'If there's one person on this planet I don't want to see tonight, it's him.'

'He's probably up at the Teletubby house with Jake,' Emma pointed out, as the taxi turned into her drive. 'Checking he's OK. You have to admit, it was nice of him to drive him home.'

'There's something about that guy I don't like,' George muttered. 'He's so full of himself.'

Emma decided not to pursue the matter.

'Aren't you coming in?' she asked as George clambered out of the car.

He shook his head. 'I'm knackered,' he said. 'And besides, I want to see how Mum and Dad are doing. I get the feeling Dad's not as well as he's trying to make out.'

'He's just tired,' Emma said.

'I hope that's all it is.' George sighed. 'So – see you tomorrow morning, yes? Half past eight?'

'You what?'

'Emma, Harriet can't work with a dodgy ankle, can she?' he reasoned. 'And we've got four rooms booked this weekend. Beds to get ready, flowers to do, tea trays to organise.'

'But your mum . . .' She caught sight of George's expression and changed her mind. 'OK.' She nodded. 'Will do. Wish me luck with Harriet.'

'You don't need luck, Blob,' he said. 'You need a bit more common sense. And a bit less nosiness about other people's business.'

He gave a twenty pound note to the taxi driver and strode off across the drive towards Donwell.

Emma stared after him. There was only one thing that stopped her being gutted by his words. He'd called her Blob. And much as she'd always hated the nickname, there was something rather comforting about that tonight.

❧ CHAPTER 8 ❧

Daring dream:
Somehow making it all come right

EMMA KNOCKED ON HARRIET'S DOOR, FEELING SLIGHTLY
sick. 'Harriet? Are you awake?'

She didn't wait for a reply but peeped round the door.
Harriet was sitting up in bed, flicking through a copy of
Heaven Sent magazine.

'I'm so sorry,' Emma blurted out. 'It's all my fault.'

'Don't be silly,' Harriet said. 'It wasn't as if you pushed
me off the breakwater, was it? Anyway, it's not broken.'
She stuck her foot out of the bedclothes and showed off
her bandaged ankle.

'A few days and it'll be fine,' she said. 'Thank goodness
– imagine if I was hobbling at the Regatta Ball!'

Emma's stomach lurched at the excitement in
Harriet's voice.

'How did you get home?' Emma asked hurriedly, if
only to delay the moment of truth. 'Who brought you?'

'You will never guess! Freddie and Jake!'

Emma was dumbfounded. 'Freddie? Jake? But how? I
mean, why?'

Harriet tossed the magazine on one side and hitched herself up on to the pillows. 'Well, I had just been discharged and collected these painkillers . . .' She gestured to a packet of analgesics by the bed. '. . . and I was hobbling out to get a taxi and these three guys came up behind me and started calling out things like . . . well, I can't even say what they were calling out.' Harriet had turned a livid shade of pink and was picking at the corner of the duvet cover. 'I tried ignoring them, and I prayed that a taxi would come up Eastern Avenue and then one of them put his arms round me and . . .' She paused. 'It was horrible, I was so scared and then guess what? A car pulled up and Freddie jumped out and he yelled at the guys that he was calling the police and they ran off.'

'Thank God for that! Oh Harriet, you've had an awful evening. And now Theo —'

She checked herself just in time. Luckily, Harriet did not appear to have heard.

'Freddie was really sweet,' she said. 'And Jake made a real fuss of me too, made me sit in the back with my leg up and kept telling Freddie to drive slowly so I didn't jar my ankle.'

'That was kind, especially as he was feeling ill himself,' Emma admitted.

'Ill? He didn't seem ill,' Harriet said. 'Not the way he was polishing off a double burger and fries!'

'That's weird, because . . .'

'And Theo? Did Theo get back OK?' Harriet asked anxiously.

Emma opened her mouth to confess everything and

changed her mind. After all, she might not have to tell the whole, horrible truth. Now that Theo knew he had no chance with her, he might, just possibly, decide that Harriet wasn't so bad after all. And that way no one would lose face. Especially her.

A night of tossing and turning proved to her how shallow those thoughts had been. As if she would want her friend to be treated as second best! At seven o'clock, she heard the loo flush in Harriet's en suite. Still in her pyjamas and bare-footed, she padded along the landing to the guest bedroom.

'Harriet, I've got something to tell you.' She knew that, now the time had come, she couldn't beat about the bush. 'About Theo.'

The way Harriet's eyes lit up and her cheeks flushed pink almost broke Emma's heart.

'Yes?' Harriet breathed eagerly.

'Something terrible has happened,' Emma began.

'To Theo? Is he ill? Has he been hurt?'

It was the genuine concern in Harriet's voice that did it for Emma. Theo Elton didn't deserve – never had deserved – someone as sweet and caring as Harriet.

'No, he's fine. It's just that – I've made the most awful mistake. I really thought he was dead keen on you, otherwise I would never have pushed you together and . . .'

'And . . . he's not?'

Emma took a deep breath. 'Last night, after that bastard had left you at the hospital all on your own, he came over to the club and he told me – Harriet, it's me he fancies, not you. I'm so so sorry.'

For what seemed like an eternity, Harriet didn't speak.

'Do you hate me?' Emma whispered.

Harriet swallowed hard. 'Of course I don't,' she replied. 'I mean, I know you thought that he liked me and, well, I was beginning to think you were right, but to be honest – well, he was never going to want someone like me, was he? I'm not nearly classy enough or . . .'

'You are far too good for him,' Emma stressed. 'And if I hadn't been so blind, I would have seen that ages ago.'

'And – are you and Theo – well, seeing one another?'

'Get real! Me and that jerk? No way. You and me are going to do one thing from this moment on. We're going to forget that Theo Elton ever existed.'

Emma's fury over Theo was further increased half an hour later when she stopped at the office to pick up the new menu cards and found him stuffing papers into the shredder. It took a few moments for her to realise just what it was that he was destroying.

'Hang on – that's my picture!' she cried.

'They're all your pictures,' he grunted. 'See?' He chucked the remaining photographs at her.

'You at the night club, you sitting in the rose garden, you giving me the come on – look.'

'How dare you!' Emma shouted, throwing them back at him. 'I didn't ask you to take these. And as for coming on to you, I wouldn't do that to Harriet.'

'Oh, so I'm good enough for your precious friend, but not good enough for you, right?' Theo thundered, shredding the last few pictures, picking up his laptop case and pushing past her. 'Well, stuff you!' With that, he stormed into the hall, leaving Emma to contemplate, just a mite guiltily, his penultimate remark.

It took a few moments before she realised that he hadn't left. His clipped tones could be heard through the office door, along with a high-pitched girly sort of giggle that certainly – to Emma's utmost relief – wasn't Harriet's.

When she peered round the door, she was taken aback to see Theo, his anger apparently evaporated, leaning against the wall chatting to a petite, auburn-haired girl who was clutching a Dictaphone and a spiral notepad.

'Can I help you?' Emma asked, cutting in on their conversation. 'Emma Woodhouse, Guest Relations Manager.'

'She wishes,' muttered Theo.

'Hi, I'm Miranda,' the girl said, proferring an immaculately manicured hand. '*Cheerio!* magazine. I was Feature Writer of the Year last year.'

Get you, thought Emma.

'I've come to see Tarquin Tee about Split Bamboo. He said to meet him at The Lodge, but I couldn't find the address.'

'Not the lodge, his eco-lodges,' Emma corrected her. 'I'll take you.'

'I'll show Miranda the way,' Theo broke in. 'I was just leaving anyway.'

'No, I can . . .'

'I'm sure, as Guest Relations Manager, you have more important things to attend to,' Theo snapped. 'Come on, Miranda – it's just across the lane.'

Emma was about to tell him where to go when she heard the back door slam and Harriet's voice greeting Mrs P in the kitchen.

'OK, bye!' she said hastily, ushering Theo and Miranda to the door. 'You'd better hurry – Dad hates to be kept waiting.'

Just seconds later, the kitchen door opened, and Harriet hobbled in, wincing slightly.

'I thought I heard Theo's voice.' Harriet was so agitated that Emma could almost see her heart beating under her T-shirt.

'Really?' Emma frowned. 'How odd. The mind plays strange tricks, doesn't it? Has Mrs P made any of her cinnamon rolls?'

For the next few days, Emma did her best to cheer Harriet up. It wasn't easy. When she lent Harriet DVDs to watch while she was working, she would find her in tears because of a love scene, or because the hero liked the same brand of lager as Theo drank. Every magazine that Emma produced to keep Harriet occupied while resting her foot seemed to feature articles headlined *The Guy Who Broke My Heart* or *Will I Ever Find True Love?*, and the fact that Theo didn't turn up all weekend, far from helping the situation, made Harriet even more despondent.

'Just to see him once more would be . . .'

'Disastrous!' declared Emma on Sunday evening, as Harriet sat listlessly in the kitchen fiddling with her mobile phone. 'What are you doing?'

'Trying to pluck up the courage to delete Theo's texts,' Harriet admitted. 'There's no point saving them now, is there?'

'So go on, do it,' Emma urged.

'I will. Later.' Harriet promised, and promptly burst into tears.

It was, thought Emma, going to be a very long week.

To: Lucyinthesky@hotmail.com
From: EmmaWH@talktalk.net

Sorry I missed your call. Was giving Harriet a pedicure in the hope of cheering her up. Am trying to think of someone I can fix her up with to take her mind of Theo. Do you think Simon W might be OK? I mean, he's a loser but . . . no that wouldn't work, would it? He's such a snob. Will Dutton? Too sporty which she's not. How about Alex Fisher? He's on his own what with Camilla hooking up with Lysander. He's the one, do you think? I so need your advice.
   Hugs, Emma.

To: EmmaWH@talktalk.net
From: Lucyinthesky@hotmail.com

So what about 'I'm never going to organise anyone's life ever again'? Forget Alex Fisher – I saw him snogging Chelsea last week at Mango's and she certainly wasn't fighting him off. Anyway, there will be loads of fit guys at F's party; maybe you can suss the right one for H then. Or even let her find her own?!! By the way, did you see how Lily and Ravi were getting it together at the club? And he's not even the best looking of the band. Weird! Talk later.
   Hugs, Lucy.

The band! Emma flipped the lid of her laptop shut and

punched the air. Emma, you're so dim, she admonished herself. The band! Why didn't I think of them before? Now, which one for Harriet?

She was still weighing up their individual attributes later that Monday morning when she found Harriet disconsolately cleaning table silver while poring over a pile of magazines, all of which were open at the horoscope page.

'You are not into all that rubbish, surely?' Emma protested.

'No, of course not,' Harriet said, guiltily shoving the magazines to one side. 'I mean, it's ridiculous isn't it – not every Pisces is going to have a disastrous month, right?'

'Exactly,' Emma said. 'Now then, I was going to ask you about the band. What do you think of the guys?'

'They're cute,' Harriet replied. 'Especially Dylan. I love guys with squashed noses. And when I got the guys' autographs, he was telling me this really funny joke – he's got this wicked laugh and —'

'So you like him the best?'

'I guess. Why?'

'No reason,' Emma assured her. 'Must dash.'

'Emma?'

'Yes?'

'It is all rubbish, this horoscope stuff, right?'

'Of course, why?'

Harriet looked close to tears. 'Because Theo's a Scorpio and it says that Scorpios are going to find true love next week.' She sighed. 'With a Leo. And I'm Pisces. But if it's all rubbish, maybe . . .'

'Harriet, Theo is a waste of space, OK? You wait – love for you is literally just around the corner. Trust me.'

It was Tarquin who managed to divert Harriet's attention, at least for a few hours, from the subject of unrequited love. Ever since Miranda had done what she called a 'taster piece' about the band for the next edition of *Cheerio!* and promised to give them full coverage in return for access to the Churchill party, Emma's father had been on a high.

'Max and Sara are delighted,' he told Emma. 'Photographs of their place are just what they need; the more publicity they can get the better.'

His delight was further increased when the producer of *Going Green* decided that he wanted to ask local people about their efforts to protect the environment, and he was particularly keen to interview young people.

'Your daughter, for instance?' he had suggested to Tarquin.

'Not a good idea,' he had said. 'She is living proof that it's nature not nurture that forms one's character. But Harriet Smith – now that's another story altogether.'

Which was how Harriet found herself, after two hours being dressed, undressed, combed and made up by Emma, and then redressed by the wardrobe people in an organic, Fair Trade cotton kaftan, sitting on the Sussex oak (local, fully sustainable) garden bench in view of the willow hurdle fencing, being questioned about recycling.

'Do you think,' she asked Emma, when the crew had finally got the takes they wanted, 'that Theo will see me on TV? Where do you think he is? He hasn't been around ever since . . .'

'Actually,' Emma said, 'he sent a text to George. He's not coming back to work on the website. He's met up with a friend who's got a yacht moored at the Marina.'

'A girl? Or a guy?'

'Haven't a clue,' Emma replied briskly. 'And does it matter? What is Theo Elton to you?'

Emma had to wait rather longer than she had hoped before Harriet replied, so softly that she could hardly hear her, 'Nothing.'

Things hotted up a lot in the run-up to Freddie's party weekend.

On the Tuesday morning, Harriet's father, who had been conspicuous by his absence, suddenly called her mobile as she and Emma were strolling back from the spa with crinkled skin, having spent an hour in the jacuzzi reading gossip magazines.

'He's found a flat,' Harriet told Emma, after talking to him in hushed tones for over ten minutes. 'He wants me to go and help him settle in.'

'And you told him where to go?'

'Emma, I can't. I mean, whatever he's done, he *is* my father.' Harriet sighed. 'And he doesn't cope well. Besides, he wants to go and visit Mum – there's a first time for everything, and he won't go alone. The thing is, I'm going to have to go over there for a few days. I'll ask George, of course – but could you cover for me? Please?'

Since there were no bookings and nothing to do

except prepare for the party, Emma felt able to be accommodating.

'Of course,' she said, squeezing Harriet's hand. 'But you will be back by Thursday, won't you? Freddie's mates are arriving during the evening.'

'Promise,' Harriet said. 'Is Theo coming then?'

'HARRIET!'

'Sorry.'

'Emma? Is that you?'

Emma turned up the volume on her mobile and stuck a finger in her left ear to blot out the sound of her father's rendition of 'Lucy in the Sky with Diamonds'.

'Hi, Freddie! How's it going?'

'That,' he replied, 'depends on you.'

Emma's heart gave a little lurch. This was the closest he'd ever got to a chat-up line.

'Really?'

'I need rescuing.' He laughed. 'I've been invited to the Bateses for lunch.'

'How on earth did you let that happen?'

'Jake's aunt said that Lily was a fan of my adverts,' he went on, and Emma could detect the note of amused pride in his voice. 'She asked Jake to invite me because she said it would make Lily's day. Apparently she's making fish pie and baked something or other. What could I say?'

'Not a lot, I guess, but what's it got to do with me?'

'Well, I told Mrs Bates that I couldn't go because I was having lunch with you and she said . . .'

'Invite darling Emma too,' Emma concluded.

'The very words!' Freddie laughed again. 'Will you?'

Despite the thought of two hours of Lily's non-stop babbling and a plateful of fish pie which, at the best of times, was not Emma's favourite meal, she only hesitated long enough to sow a tiny seed of anxiety in Freddie's mind.

'Sure I'll come,' she said. 'But you owe me one.'

'Anything!' he replied.

Oh great, thought Emma.

'Oh my God, Emma! I am so excited – you'll never guess what Jake's just done!'

Lily Bates burst into the kitchen at Donwell, where Emma was having a coffee with George's mum and Mrs P. It was Luigi's day off, which meant Mrs P had a smile on her face and there was a plate of freshly baked scones on the table.

'Oh, sorry, Mrs Knightley, I didn't know you were in here. I'll go . . . that is, I can't because I need to check on the recipes for the roulades I'm making for the party, but I guess I could do that later.'

'It's fine, Lily.' George's mum smiled. 'I was just leaving anyway. I have to take Max for a check-up.'

'He's a very funny colour if you ask me,' Mrs P observed. 'Not that I'm surprised. All that pasta stuff Luigi feeds you with. Now what he needs is one of my chicken and leek pies and a nice baked apple to follow.'

'That would be lovely.' Mrs Knightley nodded, smiling as she caught Emma's eye. Mrs P didn't believe in any rubbish about summer being a time for salads and grilled salmon. 'I'll leave it with you, Mrs P. Chicken pie sounds just the job.'

Mrs P beamed happily, hitched up her vast bosom and marched off to retrieve a chicken from the deep freeze.

'What was it you wanted exactly?' Emma asked.

'Oh yes – it's so amazing! Jake's invited . . .'

'Freddie to lunch.' Emma sighed, glancing at her watch. 'And me too – I'd better go and get ready.'

'No, not that,' Lily burst out. 'I mean, yes that too, and it's lovely you're coming. Mum's going to open the bottle of wine your dad gave her – well, she's not going to open it, obviously, with her hands, I'll do that bit, but you know what I mean.'

'So what were you going to say about Jake?'

'Oh, yes – he's invited me to Freddie's party! I mean, the party proper, not just working in the kitchen. Although, of course, I'll be in the kitchen to start with, well for the canapés and starters, but then . . .'

'But it's up to Freddie who he invites, not Jake!' Emma snapped. That guy was getting ideas above his station in life.

'Oh. You think . . .? Well, I just thought Freddie must have said . . . Oh.'

'Jake's going to be there because he's part of the band,' Emma said as patiently as she could. 'Not because he's suddenly in charge of the guest list.'

Seeing how embarrassed Lily looked, she smiled. 'But I guess you'll get to hang around anyway, won't you? It'll take ages to serve the food and clear up and —'

'Yeah. Of course. Anyway, see you at lunch.'

For reasons she couldn't begin to work out, Emma felt uncomfortable for the rest of the morning.

* * *

Before she had reached Keeper's Cottage, Emma's ears were assailed by the reverberations of an electric guitar pumping out through the open windows.

'Come in, door's open!' Mrs Bates shouted as Emma tapped on the owl-shaped door knocker.

'Was it from your dad? Was it?' Lily cried, as Jake paused in his playing and looked anxiously at Emma.

'Was what from my dad?'

'The guitar – it came today!' Lily told her. 'For Jake. Only we don't know who sent it.'

Emma bristled. 'Well, I'm certain it wasn't my father,' she said. Like he'd really lash out money on an upstart guitarist with an inflated ego.

'Me too,' Freddie nodded. 'We've been trying to work it out. Apparently, it's a very good one. Got a five-position magnetic pick-up selector, whatever that is, and a rosewood something or other.'

'Fingerboard,' Jake said, laughing. 'I mean, it's seriously top of the range.'

'Well,' Freddie teased, turning to Emma. 'I reckon Jake's got some secret admirer that he's not letting on about, some besotted fan . . .'

'Get real,' Lily said. 'How would a fan know to send the present here?'

Freddie shrugged. 'The mystery deepens,' he said. 'Maybe it's a rich girlfriend he's got hidden away, someone he's secretly meeting in the depths of the night.'

'Have you, Jake? Oh go on, admit it, you have, haven't you? That's so lovely, so romantic. You know, after Caroline and all . . .' Lily gabbled.

'Lily, shut it.' Jake put the guitar to one side. 'I guess

it's from my folks – Mum can't recall her own name sometimes, let alone remember to put a letter in with it.'

'There you are, problem solved.' Freddie grinned. 'Now – when do we eat?'

'You don't really buy that business about the guitar being from his family, do you?' Freddie murmured to Emma after lunch, while Jake and Lily were in the garden with Mrs Bates.

'Haven't thought about it,' Emma admitted, edging closer to him. If she was going to carry out her plan of seduction, now seemed as good a time as any.

'Well, you know he split with his girlfriend,' Freddie went on. 'I reckon it's from her. She's seriously wealthy, and I guess she's trying to woo him back – she knows music's his thing.'

'Do you know this girl, then?'

'Caroline? She's on the same course as me at uni,' he explained. 'That's why Split Bamboo played at the May Ball – she was on the organising committee.'

'So how come they split up?' Emma asked.

'Ah, well – that's the mystery,' said Freddie with a smile. 'My theory is that Jake's got his eye on someone else.'

'Maybe he'll bring whoever it is to the party,' Emma suggested. 'After all, he appears to be issuing invitations right, left and centre.'

'What do you mean?'

Emma told him about Lily's ridiculous idea.

'I told Jake to invite her,' Freddie said. 'You didn't seriously think I'd ignore the cousin of —'

He broke off as the others came back into the cottage.

'Talk later.' As he whispered in her ear, his lips brushed her cheek. Emma felt a frisson of anticipation ripple through her body.

'Yes, let's,' she said as huskily as she could.

On Tuesday evening, Lucy, Adam and Emma were sitting on the terrace at Donwell with George, spooning Häagen-Dazs ice cream down their throats and running through the final plans for the party. The marquee was being erected on the lawn in front of them, matting had been laid as walkways and fairy lights were being strung through all the trees leading to the house.

'We're going to have flares on the path from the house to the marquee,' Emma enthused. 'And chocolate and gold ribbons – chocolate, get it? – on the tables and . . .'

'And it's time Freddie gave us some more money,' George broke in. 'The deposit's been used up and, now Mum's back doing the books, she's keeping a very close watch on it all.'

Emma smugly handed him an envelope, slightly stained with Cookies and Cream ice cream. 'Freddie gave it to me today,' she said. 'Another thousand pounds. Happy now?'

'Wow!' Lucy exclaimed. 'Imagine having that kind of money. That's more than I'll earn all summer.'

'It better not be,' Emma said, laughing. 'We need more than that to get round Australia.'

It was the lack of a reply, together with the guilty glance that flashed between Adam and Lucy, that set

Emma's stomach churning. Lucy was going to back out. She couldn't. She wouldn't do a thing like that to her best friend. She was just worried about the cash, that was all.

'OK, so can we check numbers?' George cut in briskly. 'Luigi's nagging Mum about quantities for the food.'

'Freddie's invited fifty,' Emma said. 'But only eighteen are staying at the hotel.'

'And these are our friends – the ones who can come,' Lucy added hurriedly, clearly grateful for the change of subject.

Emma scanned the names. 'Alice, Angus, Serena, Tabitha, Chelsea, Simon – oh yuck . . .'

'He really likes you,' Lucy murmured. 'And besides, he invited us to that sailing party, remember?'

'Rufus, Candy – gosh are those two still together? Weird.' Emma went on, ignoring her. 'Maddy, Greg, Theo . . . you are so not inviting him!'

'Hang on,' Adam said laughing. 'You were the one who insisted that he got an invitation, remember? For Harriet's sake.'

'Well, things have changed and you'll just have to un-invite him,' Emma declared. 'No way is that guy setting foot —'

'You can't stop him now,' George reasoned. 'I know he's acted like a jerk, but he is a mate of mine and —'

'You have strange taste in friends,' Emma grumbled. 'Still, I guess it's too late to do anything about it. Let's just hope Harriet can hack it.'

❧ CHAPTER 9 ❧

Secret scheme:
Find out what the hell is going on

'EMMA, DARLING, LOOK WHO'S HERE!' TARQUIN BURST into the kitchen at Hartfield while Emma was still polishing off her breakfast smoothie.

'Thalia!' Emma jumped up and gave Freddie and Adam's granny a hug.

'Emma, sweetheart, how are you?' Thalia plopped down on the nearest chair and kicked off her shoes. 'I was just on my way next door with these.'

She patted a bubble-wrapped parcel of pictures. George's parents allowed Thalia to display the work of local artists on the walls of the dining room; as Max said, it covered up the dirty marks on the wallpaper and gave people something to talk about.

'It's lovely to see you,' Emma said, and meant it. Thalia was the sort of person Emma hoped she would be when she was ancient: she didn't care what anyone else thought and yet she had the kindest heart in the world. The one thing Emma didn't aspire to was Thalia's dress sense, or lack of it; it was eccentric in the extreme. On this occasion, she was wearing a calf-length patchwork skirt, a crochet top that would have made an excellent tea cosy and a pair of bright pink wellington boots. The whole outfit was topped off with a fraying straw sunhat, which sported three silk roses and a hatpin that would have come in handy for skewering kebabs.

'You might not say that when you hear the favour I need from you,' she said, laughing. 'Do those biscuits need eating?' Without waiting for a reply, she pulled the lid off the biscuit tin and began chomping on a chocolate digestive.

'It's this wretched business with Freddie,' she went on. 'No doubt you've heard.'

'What exactly?' Emma queried, her antennae for gossip coming into play.

'The argument with his father.' Thalia sighed. 'Such silliness. He told you why, I take it?'

Emma shook her head. 'No – no one knows, not even Adam,' she replied.

'What? Oh, this is stupidity, sheer and utter stupidity!' She grabbed another biscuit and bit into it angrily. 'I'll have to have a word with that boy, and soon,' she muttered. 'Of course, if his mother were here . . . but she's motorbiking across Mexico with that ridiculous husband of hers. As if her son wasn't more important!'

'Coffee, Thalia?' Tarquin asked, proffering the cafetière. 'It's Fair Trade from Venezuela, very pungent.'

'Darling, I don't care if it's come from the moon as long as it's heaped with caffeine,' Thalia said. 'Now what was I saying? Oh yes, Freddie. I have a plan and that's where you come in, Emma, dear.'

'Me?'

'Yes, dear, I want you to look after the gallery for a couple of hours while I pop up to . . . well, never mind where. What you don't know you can't lie about. Tarquin, these biscuits are most frightfully good. It would be such a shame to let them go stale.'

'Help yourself,' he replied. 'Look, I must fly – I'm seeing a man about solar-powered water heaters. By the way, Thalia, that gallery of yours is a disgrace – you have lights on all day.'

'I'll have you know I bought an energy-saving bulb yesterday,' Thalia countered. 'Silly shape though, not aesthetic at all.'

She waved Tarquin out of the door as if she owned the place and turned to Emma. 'Now,' she said, 'we must go. If this is going to work, timing is everything.'

Wealden Art Gallery stood in the middle of Ditchdean High Street, between the Copper Kettle tearoom and the fifteenth-century Priest's House, and as a consequence there were always tourists gawping through the window at the pictures and ceramics on display. Few, however, ventured through the door and even fewer made a purchase, beyond the odd postcard or calendar of *Sussex through the Seasons*.

'Now dear,' Thalia said, unlocking the door and turning the *Closed* sign to *Open*. 'All you have to do is answer the phone, smile invitingly at anyone who sets foot across the threshold and should my grandson appear, spin him some yarn about my going to the dentist or some such and get rid of him fast, OK?'

'Is Freddie likely to appear?' Emma tried to keep the eagerness out of her voice.

'I wasn't thinking about Freddie, I meant Adam,' Thalia replied, eyeing Emma closely. 'Tell me, you haven't got a thing about Freddie, have you?'

'Me? No – I just meant . . .' To her annoyance, Emma felt her cheeks burn.

'Hmm.' Thalia sniffed and picked up her outsize handbag. 'Well, just don't . . . I mean . . . oh, I just don't want you to get hurt.'

'I won't,' Emma assured her. 'Why do I have to get rid of him if he comes?'

'That guy on *England Today* was right,' Thalia remarked. 'The young ask too many questions. Just do it.' And with that, she disappeared out of the door.

Emma had just begun to feel bored – there's only so much excitement to be gained from selling two Sussex by the Sea pencils and a postcard of Ditchdean Beacon – when the door opened and Freddie sauntered in with Jake following close behind.

They both looked extremely surprised to see her.

'What are you doing here?' Freddie exclaimed, glancing around the empty gallery. 'Where's Granny?'

'Er – she's at the dentist,' Emma replied hastily. 'Toothache. Really bad.' She glanced surreptitiously at her watch. 'What did you want her for?'

'What? Oh, nothing really,' Freddie said. 'Just wanted her advice about something.'

It occurred to Emma that, for the first time ever, he wasn't his confident, assured self.

'Can I do something?' she offered.

Jake glanced at Freddie. 'Shall we tell her?' he ventured. 'If she knows, it's going to make life a whole heap easier.'

'Tell her about Ravi, you mean? Sure.' Freddie laughed, turning to Emma. 'Know what? Ravi's really got the hots for Jake's cousin.'

'Freddie, that's a bit unfair,' Jake began.

'For Lily?' Emma was incredulous. She'd always thought of Lily as the least likely girl on the planet to pull a guy.

'The thing is,' Freddie went on, 'Ravi's dead shy. I mean, seriously buttoned up. That's right, isn't it, Jake?'

Jake sighed and nodded. 'Yeah and he's not the only one,' he muttered under his breath.

'So if you can drop the hint to Lily, suss out how she feels about him . . .'

He paused as the telephone on the desk rang.

'Wealden Art Gallery, Emma Woodhouse speaking, how may I help you?'

'Emma? Thalia. I'm ten minutes away – is the coast clear?'

'Ah. Not really,' Emma mumbled. 'It will be very soon. OK, then. Bye!'

'That was, er, the firework people,' she gabbled. 'They need you up at the hotel to check out – stuff.'

Freddie frowned. 'Surely George can do that?'

'George isn't around,' Emma said. 'And from what they said, there's a problem with . . . something. It's urgent.'

'OK, no sweat, we'll go up there,' Freddie said, opening the door on to the street. 'And find out whether Lily likes Ravi, OK? Oh, and when Granny gets back, can you tell her we were here? To discuss what she was talking about?'

'Sure – what was that exactly?'

'She'll understand,' Freddie assured her.

I'm glad someone will, thought Emma. Something was clearly going on, and she had every intention of finding out exactly what it was.

'Emma, you're a star,' Thalia exclaimed ten minutes later. 'Now, off you go.'

'It's OK, I'm not in any rush,' Emma assured her. 'I could help you hang those if you like.' She gestured to a pile of screen prints stacked in the corner of the gallery.

'No, darling, it's sweet of you but, well, to be honest, I need some space. Down time, you know? So off you pop.'

She wants rid of me, thought Emma. She's positively buzzed. I wonder if she's got a secret lover, and that's where she's been. Eyeing Thalia's crêpe-like neck and the age spots on her slender hands, she dismissed the thought as ridiculous.

'Oh, Freddie was here, with Jake,' Emma told her as Thalia held the door open for her. 'He said he needed advice and you'd know what it was about.'

'Oh, I know all right.' Thalia sighed. 'And hopefully after this weekend, he'll come to his senses and all this stupidity will be over.'

She blew a kiss at Emma and almost kicked her out of the door.

* * *

'Emma! There's no sign of anyone from the firework suppliers,' Freddie declared the moment Emma set foot inside Donwell. 'Are you sure you got the message right?'

'Actually, I lied,' she admitted. 'We've got a surprise for you, at the party, and the phone call was about that, and I had been sworn to secrecy and so — '

Freddie laughed. 'Wow! What is it? A strippergram? A Morgan convertible? Outsize chocolate fountain?'

'Wait and see,' Emma, who was no wiser than he was, replied. 'Now if you don't mind, I've got to find Lily. I'll report back once I've sussed her out on my love-o-meter!'

'How do you feel about Ravi?'

Emma didn't see any point wasting time in getting to the point.

Lily paused in between slicing carrots.

'Ravi?' she repeated, blushing slightly. 'I don't really know him. I mean, we talked at the club that night. Guess what? His mother's sister used to do my mother's hair before we moved house and his brother's girlfriend is the niece of my home ec tutor.'

'Lily, I'm not interested in his family tree. I want to know if you fancy him.'

'Well, kind of.'

'Can you elaborate on "kind of"?' Emma persisted.

'I've never had a boyfriend.' Lily sighed. 'Not a proper one. I've been out with a couple of guys but they never hang around long.'

Clearly guys with taste, thought Emma.

'So, if Ravi asked you out?'

'Well, I'd go of course,' Lily said. 'He's really interesting – he wants to go back to Bangladesh and teach music to kids who can't afford lessons or instruments. If the band's CDs make money, he'll set up a charity. He was explaining about —'

'If you fancy him, come on to him at the party,' Emma ordered. 'Do something with your hair, get a sexy outfit, pluck your eyebrows and go for it.'

'But . . .'

'Lily, apparently he's dead keen on you. Strange, I know, but true. So go for it. You might not get another chance with him.' Maybe, she thought again for the millionth time, she should take Lily in hand. Then again, she'd never manage to cope with her juvenile ways. There were limits, even for her.

Harriet arrived back at Emma's house on a real high, out of all proportion for someone whose father had apparently rented a grotty flat above a fish and chip shop.

'He's really turned over a new leaf,' Harriet said. 'He says he's going to get a proper job and never go inside a betting shop again. And I really think he means it this time.'

'People don't change their personality types,' Emma told her wisely. 'It's in my *Psychology for the Real World* book. So don't get your hopes up.'

'Oh come on, you have to hope, don't you?' Harriet insisted. 'Anyway, I'm too happy to worry about stuff like that. Guess what happened yesterday?'

'Wouldn't it be quicker for you simply to tell me?' Emma teased.

'I bumped into Libby and Rob,' she said triumphantly. 'It was so cool – we went to Caffé Nero and she treated us all to lattes and muffins.'

'Lovely,' murmured Emma.

'And Rob said he misses me,' Harriet went on. 'He misses me so much that, guess what?'

'Harriet . . .'

'Sorry,' she said with a laugh. 'He's going to ask George for a job here!'

Emma's mouth dropped open. 'He can't do that,' she cried. 'He's got a job. Of sorts.'

'Yes, but that's in the daytime,' Harriet said. 'He thought he might get work in the bar in the evenings and Sundays. And I said that, with the party and all, we could do with more help.' She paused, watching Emma closely. 'George did say that those evening wedding receptions next week would be a pain without the right staff. It was all right to say that, wasn't it?' she asked anxiously.

'Well,' Emma said, shrugging. 'Let's hope Max and Sara think so. I mean, you've put them in a really awkward position, haven't you?'

'I have? How come?'

'If they don't think Rob is suitable – and after all, they have very high standards and I doubt he's clued up about silver service – then he's going to feel let down and inadequate, all because of you. Poor guy, his self-esteem would take a real bashing.'

'Oh no, I never thought of it like that. I'll ring him – I'll say I got it wrong. I'll say there are no vacancies. That should do it.'

'I think that's very kind,' Emma replied gently. 'That's the most loving thing you can do.'

❧ CHAPTER 10 ❧

Daring dream:
Seduce A-list guy, dispose of C-list tart

Even George's father had brightened considerably by Friday. The arrival of Freddie's guests the previous evening, the sight of Morgans and Porsches and a particularly stylish silver Mercedes coupe parked in his drive and the thwack of croquet mallets on the south lawn, restored his bonhomie and gave him the feeling that Donwell Abbey was what it had once been: one of the true ancestral piles of Old England.

Mrs Knightley, who was more of a realist and had four times as much work to do, just smiled and removed the Glenmorangie to an even safer hiding place.

To begin with, Emma was in her element. At least three times in the preceding week, Freddie had told her she was a genius and, although she knew it was true, it was good to hear the trace of adoration in his voice as she explained how she'd set up venues for quad biking, horse riding, paragliding and skateboarding as well as the archery, golf, fishing, and clay-pigeon shooting on offer in the grounds. On Thursday evening, everyone had chosen their activity and there had been a lot of 'oohs' and 'aahs' over breakfast on Friday when Emma and Harriet dished out the individual picnic hampers stuffed with smoked salmon and cucumber mousse, cold chicken, strawberries and, most importantly, a quarter bottle of champagne.

After breakfast, Freddie instigated the singing of 'For She's a Jolly Good Fellow' in praise of Mrs P's kedgeree, which he declared was the best this side of the Indian Ocean and as result Mrs P was now putty in his hands and determined to provide the best afternoon tea that Donwell had ever seen.

It was as everyone was piling into the mini jeeps that George had hired on Freddie's instructions that Emma saw something that threatened to ruin her entire day: Theo Elton was strolling up the drive, hand in hand with Miranda, the reporter from *Cheerio!*

'What the hell is he doing here?' she hissed at George. 'He's only invited to the party.'

'Ah,' murmured George.

'What's "Ah" supposed to mean?' demanded Emma.

'Theo phoned and asked for Freddie's mobile number . . .'

'And you gave it to him? How stupid can you get?' Emma exploded. 'Anyway, that doesn't answer my question.'

'He was just ringing to ask whether he could bring his new girlfriend.'

'*Girlfriend?*' Emma spluttered. 'They only met a few days ago and besides it was me he was in love with!'

'You didn't want him,' George pointed out.

'That's not the point,' Emma snapped. 'How do you think Harriet is going to feel?' She glanced over her shoulder, grateful that Harriet and Lily were fully occupied in the kitchen. 'You should never have let Freddie agree to them coming.'

'Oh, Emma, come off it,' George protested. 'What was I supposed to do? I'm not the one footing the bill. Anyway, when he heard what Theo had to say, he couldn't get him over here quickly enough. And I must admit I was pretty keen myself.'

Emma frowned. Freddie hadn't mentioned any new developments to her and she was, after all, the party planner. Besides, George hated Freddie.

'So what was the big attraction?' she demanded.

'Miranda,' George said with a wry grin. 'She's offered to do a big piece on the band —'

'I know that, Dad told me,' Emma interrupted. 'Doesn't mean she has to be here now.'

'Oh yes, she does,' George corrected her. 'The magazine want the whole country house party thing — there's a photographer coming too. It'll be a huge spread, loads of pictures of the house and gardens, masses about our activities — and we won't have to pay a penny.'

'Oh.' Much as the sight of Theo Elton made her want to vomit, she had to admit that the Knightleys were hardly in a position to pass up on an opportunity like that.

'Emma, someone's left their picnic in the dining room!' Harriet ran into the hall, waving a hamper. 'I think it's —' She stopped dead and stared out of the open front door. 'That's Theo.' She stood open-mouthed, like a rabbit caught in headlights. And then before Emma could stop her, she was out of the front door and heading towards him.

'Now look what you've done!' Emma hissed at George. 'This is going to traumatise her big time. I hope you're satisfied.'

'Emma, do you always have to be such a drama queen?' George sighed. 'If anyone is to blame, it's you because —'

'What are you two rabbiting on about?' Freddie said as he strolled towards them. He glanced at his watch. 'George, your clay-pigeon shooting party is champing at the bit, so you'd better get over there.'

He turned to Emma. 'Are you sure you won't join us?' he asked, tipping his finger under her chin so that shivers of anticipation rippled down her spine. 'Jake and the guys are doing quad biking and I said I'd tag along for a laugh.'

'Between you and me,' George murmured, 'I can't see Emma wanting to spend her day knee deep in mud!'

'It would have been fun,' she lied, watching with increasing anxiety as Harriet tried to chat to Theo, 'but I've loads to do for the party. By the way, what are Theo and Miranda doing?'

'Horse riding,' Freddie replied.

'Let's hope he falls off,' Emma muttered under her breath. 'Preferably head first into a cow pat.'

The more Emma saw of Miranda, the more she loathed her. She was into everything, shoving her little Dictaphone under people's noses, laughing too loudly and prefacing every remark with, 'When I interviewed . . .'

and then mentioning some C-list celebrity as though speaking to them had been the journalistic coup of the year. She kept ordering Liam, the somewhat weedy and acne-ridden photographer, about and would insist on calling Emma 'Em' to which, needless to say, she refused to respond. The girl was the pits. Luckily, it seemed that Freddie wasn't particularly impressed with her either.

'I know it's great for the guys to get this publicity,' he complained to Emma on Friday evening while everyone was lounging around on the lawn drinking Pimms or setting up an impromptu game of cricket, 'but she's so in your face. And very common.'

Emma glanced over to where Miranda was chatting to Dylan and Nick; he had a point. Which made it even more strange that Theo was taking an interest in her.

'So,' she said, touching Freddie's arm lightly, 'how's it going so far? How do I rate as a party planner?'

'Top of the range,' Freddie replied.

'And,' Emma said, seductively running her tongue along her lower lip and edging closer to Freddie, 'how do I rate in other ways?'

She held her breath. Had she said too much? She could see several pairs of eyes on them. Now was not the time to get the brush off.

She exhaled in relief as Freddie cupped her face in his hands. 'You're – lovely,' he murmured, glancing over his shoulder. 'There's so much I want to say to you, but not here. Later – why don't we . . .?'

'Freddie! Over here!' Jake shouted from the other side of the lawn. 'Miranda wants to get a shot of me and the rest of the band!'

Damn Miranda, thought Emma as Freddie dropped his hands to his side. But I've got him.

'Catch you later,' he whispered, winking at her. 'OK?'

'Absolutely,' Emma said with a smile. 'I'll be waiting.'

She had a long wait. Of course, she understood why. With so many people milling around, and Thalia popping in and out, and George's parents getting into a tizz and asking her to check and double-check decorations and table plans and party favours, there was hardly a moment to draw breath, let alone have a full-on snog. But twice she caught Freddie gazing at her with a yearning expression on his face and that was enough. For now. Once the party was under way, she could think of at least three quiet corners they could disappear into. Not too quiet, of course – she needed her triumph to be witnessed by as many of her own mates as possible.

At seven o'clock on Saturday evening, Emma and Lucy were in Emma's bedroom preparing for the party. Emma was standing in front of her mirror, eyeing her fancy dress costume with a degree of smug satisfaction. The theme that Freddie had finally chosen, after a lot of input from Emma, was Beaux and Belles.

'That way, people can be as randy or as demure as they like,' Emma had told him. 'Something for everyone.'

'And which will you be? Randy or demure?' Freddie had asked, touching her arm and leaning towards her with a mischievous expression on his face,.

'You'll have to wait and see, won't you?' she had replied enigmatically.

Now, surveying her reflection in the mirror, she felt she had hit exactly the right note for what was clearly going to be an evening of intimacy. She'd gone for the Regency heroine look. The Maximum Uplift bra that she was wearing under her electric-blue ball gown enhanced her cleavage enough to be enticing yet subtle, and, as she fingered the ringlets that had taken Stephanie at Cut Above three hours and a lot of subdued swearing to achieve, she felt ready for anything that Freddie had to offer. It had, after all, taken him long enough to pluck up the courage, and it would be so unfair to disappoint him.

'Do you think I look subtly seductive?' Emma asked Lucy.

'Subtle? You?' Lucy laughed, pulling off her jeans and T-shirt. 'You'll have guys salivating before we've finished the buffet.'

'Oh good,' Emma replied. 'Only Freddie —'

'Listen, I'm not being funny, but don't go overboard. I reckon Freddie's a bit of a playboy; you know, pick a girl up, dump her, move on? Just a feeling.'

'Come off it, I'm not asking for marriage,' Emma retorted. 'Besides, he likes me. I know he does. I can sense these things.'

'Right,' Lucy said, gazing into the mirror. 'Do you think I was a bit silly going as a bathing belle? Does my bum look big in bloomers?'

By eleven o'clock, Emma knew that all her planning had been worthwhile. The party was a triumph; the marquee had been transformed into Regency Brighton, complete with a bathing machine in one corner (dispensing somewhat unRegency popcorn) and a Punch and Judy booth in another. Fishing nets and stuffed seagulls hung from the ceiling and Emma's father had managed to hire a barrel organ played by an overweight guy in a striped blazer and straw boater. Freddie, who looked divine as Beau Brummell, had danced with her three times. He'd even kissed her – only sadly it was on the top of her head, which didn't really count, but he kept muttering about getting her on her own and that did. The champagne had been flowing like water. Even George, sporting a footman's outfit, seemed happy and gave her a hug, saying that, even though she was stubborn, bossy and infuriating, she'd done a great job.

All the old school gang were having a ball – Serena and Angus had come back from Rock for the event (Emma took great satisfaction in noting that Serena's nose was peeling – had she never heard of total block?) and Tabitha, Chelsea and the rest were all competing to get the photographer from *Cheerio!* to include them in his shots. Adam was dropping the words 'my brother' into every other sentence, conveniently leaving out the 'half', and Lucy had confided in Emma that Freddie thought she was 'amazing'.

If there was anything to dampen her sense of elation, it was the sight of Harriet, who, having finished her waitressing duties, had changed into a particularly unflattering dress that she'd hired from some sleazy fancy dress shop, and was sitting in a corner tapping her feet in time to the music and trying to look as if she didn't care about being the only person who hadn't danced once. Harriet's eyes seemed to follow Theo and Miranda round the room, which was unfortunate since they were spending a great deal of time exploring the depths of one another's throat right in front of her, which Emma considered to be in very bad taste anyway. Every time Emma caught Harriet's eye, she smiled; but the smile didn't last and, as the evening wore on, Harriet seemed to be the only person who looked as if she wished she was anywhere but at Freddie's party.

'Why the long face?' George asked Emma. 'It's going well.'

'It's Harriet.' Emma sighed. 'I've got to find a guy to dance with her. Do you think Simon Wittering would do?'

'You said he was a loser,' George reminded her.

'Well, he is, but . . .' She paused remembering Theo's comments about double standards. 'Well, Tom then, or Calum – or —'

'You are unbelievable,' George said laughing. 'Rather than abandon Harriet to your totally off-the-wall matchmaking, I'm going to dance with her myself!'

Emma smiled as he walked over to Harriet, whispered in her ear and led her into the middle of the packed dance floor. He was such a sweet guy. And actually, she mused, his dancing was getting better. Much less demented chicken and more —

'Emma, come and dance?'

Freddie was at her side, his hand already under her elbow. He didn't have to ask twice.

'Look, can we find somewhere quiet?' Freddie

whispered in Emma's ear five minutes later. 'There's something I have to say to you and I can't do it here. Please?'

'Sure,' she said, trying to still the fluttering in her chest. 'Why don't we go outside?'

She was just leading him to the doorway when someone seized her arm. 'I want you to do something and do it now!' Thalia, who when Emma had last seen her, had been sitting out on the terrace with Tarquin, George's parents and a few other wrinklies, was now looking extremely excited and very flushed. 'Go and get the band to stop playing and do a drum roll.'

'I can't, we were just —'

'Granny, what's all this?' Freddie sounded irritated in the extreme. 'Back off, OK?'

'Emma, just do it!'

There was something in Thalia's tone that brooked no argument. Emma pushed her way over to the band and whispered the instructions in Ravi's ear. Being the professional he was, he took not a blind bit of notice, so she did the only thing she could. She whipped the drumsticks out of his hands. 'Drum roll – surprise – do it now!' she ordered.

'What's going on?' Jake turned, open-mouthed, to Ravi, who shrugged and glared at Emma. But by then Thalia was beside them, a very reluctant Freddie in tow.

'Right everyone,' she shouted. 'I know it's another half-hour before Freddie is actually twenty-one but what the heck? *Happy birthday to you, happy . . .*'

Whether it was because Thalia's singing was so off-key

that it needed drowning out, or simply because after copious quantities of champagne everyone's inhibitions had vanished, Emma wasn't sure, but within seconds the whole place was reverberating to singing, clapping, cheering and the odd bawdy heckle from the likes of Simon Wittering. She darted back to Freddie's side and slipped her hand in his.

'And now,' Thalia shouted, holding up a hand to still the hubbub, 'a birthday surprise!'

Ravi, having got the hang of things, beat out another drum roll.

'Oh my God!' Freddie's groan could be clearly heard by those standing near him. 'This is all I need.'

Emma saw Miranda, who was standing close by, kick Liam the photographer with her stiletto and gesture to the doorway of the marquee.

'Start shooting and don't stop!' she murmured. 'This could be big.'

Emma turned and followed Miranda's gaze. Standing in the doorway was Sir Douglas Churchill, Freddie's father.

'Happy twenty-first, Frederick,' he boomed, striding across the floor and slapping Freddie on the back as Liam flashed shot after shot. 'Good to see you.'

Despite the astonishment at seeing him there, it wasn't Sir Douglas who took Emma's attention. It was the way that Freddie's hand gripped hers so tightly that she thought her knuckles would crack, and the look of sheer panic on his face.

'Dad, what are you doing here? I mean, it's great but . . .' he stammered.

'It wasn't my idea, I confess,' he replied gruffly. 'But

your grandmother – well, we have things to clear up.'

He turned to Emma. 'And who is this delightful young lady?'

'Sorry – let me introduce you. This is Emma. Emma, darling, meet my father.'

Just for a moment, Emma was speechless, thinking, Emma, darling – he called me darling. In front of his father.

'I'm delighted to meet you, Sir Douglas,' she said, her natural good manners coming into play as the camera flashed again and again. 'How lovely that you could come.'

'Sweetheart, will you excuse us just for a minute?' Freddie asked, turning to Emma. 'I need to have a bit of time with my father.' And with that, he tipped her chin, leaned forward and kissed her full on the lips. 'Back in a minute,' he whispered and led his father away.

Emma was reeling. He had to be madly in love with her to behave like that in front of his father. The odd thing was that, now he'd actually come on strong, her heart had stopped fluttering, her legs hadn't turned to jelly and, although she was disappointed that he wasn't around to dance now the disco had started and the DJ was playing 'Catch My Heart', she soon had guys clamouring to get her on to the dance floor. She did wonder where Freddie and his father had got too, but she was more concerned to work out just how many of her mates had seen the kiss.

She was satisfied to see Tabitha and Serena nudging one another and looking enviously in her direction.

'Have you had too much to drink?' George suddenly appeared, having handed Harriet over to the tender mercies of Simon Wittering. 'What was going on with you and Freddie?'

'He kissed me,' she said calmly. 'Do you have a problem with that?'

'Me? Why should I? You're the one with the problem. I've told you, that guy is not right for you.'

'Oh really? And why's that? Because he's fit? Because he knows how to have a laugh? Because . . . Oh my God! What has Lily got on?'

Lily, her kitchen duties obviously over for the evening, was standing on tiptoe in the doorway of the marquee, waving at Emma. She was wearing an emerald green shift dress with silver bells and bows sewn all over it.

'She looks like a downmarket Christmas tree,' Emma muttered to George, as Lily pushed through the throng of dancers to reach them. 'Lily, what are you wearing?'

'What? Bows and bells,' she said. 'I thought . . . oh dear. Oh.'

Her eyes scanned the costumes in the room, the long dresses, bathing belles, dandies and, in the case of Tabitha, Belle from *Beauty and the Beast*.

'Oh no, I didn't get it – see, Jake didn't send an invitation or anything, he just said bows and bells, and I've never been to a posh do like this and I just thought . . .'

'No, you didn't think,' Emma snapped, still smarting from George's comments. 'You never do. If you'd engaged your brain for one minute – well, that presupposes there is a brain to engage . . . you'd have realised that people like Freddie's set don't do tacky. And tonight you are the queen of tack.'

Lily stared at her open-mouthed.

'Oh. You mean . . . you think . . . well, I'd better go and change. I don't know what into though, I haven't got anything glamorous . . . but if you think he'll be upset . . .'

'I think it's a great costume,' George broke in, glaring at Emma through narrowed eyes. 'Far more imaginative than all this lot. And that colour suits you perfectly.' He reached out a hand to her. 'Come on, let me get you some champagne – and there are some pretty cool king prawn kebabs lurking somewhere.'

'I'll have some more champers too,' Emma called after him, although she knew that she'd had more than enough already.

'Get your own,' he replied and kept moving.

For the next half-hour, George didn't speak to, or even look at, Emma. Lily, it seemed, was the centre of attention. Lily danced with Ravi while the band was having its break, and then with a succession of guys, none of whom seemed remotely put out by her bizarre outfit.

When Freddie eventually reappeared, Emma was at his side in an instant.

'Is everything OK? What made your dad come? Have you two made it up?'

'I'm going to kill Granny.' He sighed. 'Apparently, this is all down to her. When Pa flew in from the States, she met him at the airport, collared him and got him to agree to come down here.'

So that's where she was, Emma thought. So much for the wrinkled lover. 'But that's good, isn't it?'

'No, it's not,' Freddie retorted, shaking his head. 'He's in transit – tomorrow morning he flies to Rome and then on to Sydney, to negotiate the buyout of some confectionery outfit and he wants me to go with him.'

'Oh no!' Emma was dismayed more for herself than for him.

'He says it's only right for the heir to the Churchill Chocolates' name to be seen learning the ropes.' Freddie recited his father's words with a sneer in his voice. 'As if I give a damn for coffee creams and bloody champagne truffles!'

'So you won't go?'

Freddie ran his hand through his hair and avoided her gaze. 'I've compromised,' he muttered. 'I've said I'll go to Rome but no further.'

'But that's tomorrow,' Emma gasped. 'The weekend's not over till Monday morning.'

Freddie looked downcast. 'I know. I'm going to have to leave really early, too. But what could I do? I have to keep him sweet till, well, for the time being, anyway.' He took her hand. 'Will you sort everyone out – make sure they have a good time? Please?'

'Of course I will,' she assured him. 'For you.'

He swallowed. 'Look, I'm really sorry. I feel dreadful about everything.'

'Let's see if I can't make you feel better,' she murmured, slipping a hand into his and trying to make her eyes go all smoky and alluring. 'That quiet place we were going to is still there, you know.'

Far from looking ecstatic at the prospect, Freddie's face clouded with misery. 'Emma, I can't, not now,' he replied. 'But you're right, I really need to talk to you, to tell you how it is. Look, give me ten minutes and then —'

His mobile phone began ringing in the pocket of his tight breeches and it took him a few seconds of wriggling and manoeuvring to get it out.

'Text,' he said, flipping open the cover. His face paled. 'I don't believe this,' he moaned. 'Some birthday this is turning out to be.'

'What's wrong? What's happened?'

'Nothing that need worry you,' he said, with a faint smile. 'I'll deal with it. Later. Come on, let's —'

'Fireworks, five minutes!' George brushed past them, addressing the words to Freddie and ignoring Emma completely. 'Can you start getting people outside?'

'Will do.' Freddie broke away and headed across the marquee to the bar, where Jake and the other guys were downing beers.

'Thanks for looking after Harriet,' Emma said, following George in an attempt to make her peace. 'It was really kind of you. And Lily too . . .'

'How could you have been so horrid to her, Emma?' George demanded. 'Do you enjoy putting people down?'

'I didn't mean anything by it — she knows it was a joke.'

'Oh does she? So how come she was fighting back tears? How come she actually asked me whether she'd been an idiot ever to think you were her friend?'

'I've never treated her like a best mate . . .'

'You don't need to tell me that,' George snapped. 'I

suppose because she's not a trust-fund babe, and she spends her free time doing something worthwhile instead of bumming around with empty-headed, precocious . . .' He glared across the room at Freddie who was marshalling his friends out on to the terrace. 'You know something?' he concluded. 'Harriet would never have behaved like that. Maybe you should learn from her – instead of wasting your time trying to fix her up with one of your shallow friends.' And with that, he stormed off without a backward glance.

And Emma found herself sobbing silently as the first rocket flared into the night sky.

'Hey, what's with the tears?'

Miranda nudged Emma's arm as a cascade of silver stars burst from a firework over their heads. Her expression was mocking rather than sympathetic.

'Hay fever,' Emma snapped.

'Right, I believe you, thousands wouldn't.' Miranda laughed. 'Wouldn't have anything to do with Freddie, would it?'

'Freddie?' Emma was genuinely surprised. 'What makes you think that?'

'Theo told me what a flirt you are,' Miranda said. 'That you can't resist anything in trousers and then you dump them without a backward glance.'

'He said that? The —'

'Hey, I'm not judging you,' Miranda replied. 'Have a good time while you've got the chance, I say. But, as far as Freddie's concerned, you don't have even a glimmer of a chance.'

'Well that shows how little you know,' Emma retorted

cuttingly. 'He and I are an item. Besides, it's none of your business.'

Miranda smirked. 'Oh I think you'll find it's very much my business,' she replied. 'Still, if you don't want my help . . .'

'I don't need anyone's help with my life, thank you,' Emma replied. 'However, if you're hooking up with Theo Elton, *you're* going to need all the help you can get.'

❧ CHAPTER 11 ❧

Secret scheme:
Don't let anyone know just how much it hurts

It was two in the morning. All the evening guests had gone home, and those staying at the hotel were either in their rooms, sprawled on sofas in one of the lounges or, in the case of Ben Rigby, throwing up into the rhododendrons. Sir Douglas had departed for the Grand Hotel in Brighton, but not before posing for numerous photographs with his son and heir, two of which (at Freddie's insistence) included Emma.

The band had dismantled their gear and gone back to the lodges. Harriet, George and Lily were clearing up the worst of the mess in the marquee and Emma, anxious to steer clear of them for the time being, was looking for Freddie. She was heading for the conservatory and beginning to despair of ever finding him when she heard the murmur of voices coming from the billiard room.

The door was slightly ajar. Kicking off her shoes, she crept closer.

'Just how much longer are you going to let that guy

hijack your life?' That was Jake's voice, tight with anger.

'I'm not – it's just this once.' Freddie's voice had a note of pleading.

'You always say that,' Jake snapped. 'You've got to make a clean break.'

Emma was so incensed that she could hardly think straight. Who did Jake Fairfax think he was? Telling Freddie how to behave with his own father – it was despicable! If it hadn't been for Freddie – and her dad of course – the band would still be on the sidelines, wannabes in the music world.

'Look, I'll sort it, OK?' Freddie said. 'I'll go tomorrow, deal with him once and for all.'

'Well, if you don't do it this time . . .' Jake dropped his voice and Emma could no longer catch his words. She was edging a step closer to the gap in the door, when she heard the clatter of high heels behind her.

'Oh, there you are!' Harriet came bustling over, a broad smile on her face. 'Wasn't that just the best party you have ever been to? I've had so much fun, I can't tell you.'

'Shh,' Emma hissed but it was too late. She stepped back quickly as the door was pulled closed from the inside and the conversation became nothing more than a muffled hum.

Everyone slept late on Sunday morning. Everyone except Emma. She had slept in snatches; when she did nod off, she dreamed of George shouting at her and of Lily ripping her dress off and throwing herself into the fishpond. She dreamed she was pushing Jake in after her.

But she didn't dream of Freddie. She lay in bed and thought about him. She tried to feel like someone in love. Clearly he was in love with her, and if it hadn't been for all the interruptions he would have told her just how he felt.

But now that she'd got him eating out of her hand, did she want him? Did she really fancy a guy who would let some jumped-up guitarist tell him how to conduct his life? Was it possible that she'd allowed herself to waste time trying to pull a wimp?

The thought was so disturbing that by eight o'clock she was up and dressed and walking over to Donwell in the hope of catching Freddie before he left for the airport.

For some reason – later she thought it must have been divine intervention – she wandered into the marquee where Ray and Dave, the two gardeners from Hartfield, were already dismantling tables and taking up the matting.

'Morning, Miss Emma,' Ray called. 'Got some stuff here you might want to sort through.'

She wandered over and eyed the small pile of things on one of the tables. An eyeliner pencil, perfume atomiser, an aquamarine earring and a mobile phone.

The phone she recognised at once. It was Freddie's.

'Thanks, Ray,' she said hurriedly. 'I'll get these back to their rightful owners.'

She nipped out of the marquee and hurried down to the gazebo by the rose garden. She knew she shouldn't. She wouldn't. She mustn't.

She flipped open the cover of the phone and opened the *Messages* menu.

How can u do this 2 me? U said u wld luv me 4ever. If u don't come I'll tell everyone the truth. J.

Emma read the message for the third time. It was obviously from Judy, the girl who'd given him such grief over the nightclub thing. Freddie must have told her in no uncertain terms that it was Emma he wanted and now she was throwing the teddy out of the pram. Not that Freddie couldn't deal with hysterical adolescents.

She went into the Outbox menu, eager to find his reply.

OK, I'm coming. Meet me at usual place 9am. F

She couldn't believe her eyes. Surely he wasn't going to succumb to emotional blackmail? Besides, what was Judy expecting to tell people? That Freddie Churchill was in love with Emma Woodhouse? Who would care? Come to think of it, did she care?

She pushed that last thought from her mind and peered at the screen once more. There was only one logical explanation as to why Freddie would reply like that. He was scared that she'd do drugs again.

At least that explained his reaction; he wasn't a wimp, he was just burdened with unnecessary guilt. She needed to find him and fast and tell him that he didn't need to feel responsible for anyone, least of all an ex-girlfriend. She glanced at her watch and set off across the lawn towards the house. If she didn't hurry, he'd be on his way to the airport.

She stopped dead in her tracks. It was OK. He couldn't go after Judy – he'd promised his father. He must have sent the reply before Sir Douglas made his suggestion. Only he hadn't. The timing on the text proved that. He must have told her he would come, knowing that he couldn't. But he had promised. And you don't promise something you know you can't deliver. Or if you do, you're not a very nice person. George always said there was something about him. But then George wasn't always right. Was he?

'Has anyone seen Freddie?' Emma stuck her head round the dining room door. Lily, who was replenishing the fruit bowl, caught her eye, averted her gaze and scuttled out of the other door.

Emma would have run after her and tried to make her peace, but the matter in hand was far too important to wait.

'He left a while ago,' Miranda said. 'And I'd better get off too, if this feature's going to get into the next edition.'

'Aren't you staying for the barbecue?' Theo asked.

'No need, I've got what I came for,' she said, smiling at him. 'In spades. I just need a final word with Jake.'

'No chance he'll be up yet,' Emma replied shortly, still smarting over the conversation at the fireworks. 'They never surface till nine on a good day, let alone after a late night.'

'Oh, he'll surface for me all right,' Miranda said confidently.

'So when will it be in the magazine?' someone asked eagerly.

'Friday,' Miranda said. 'Be prepared for a real scoop. She paused, frowning. 'Theo, is that your phone ringing?'

'It's mine!' Emma lied, fingering Freddie's mobile,

which was in the pocket of her shorts. She scooted out of the room, closing the door behind her.

Pa mobile

Emma stared at the screen, not knowing what to do. If Sir Douglas was phoning, it meant Freddie wasn't with him. Which could only mean one thing: he'd gone grovelling to this Judy cow. On the other hand, maybe he was stuck in traffic; if she didn't answer and Sir Douglas didn't ring again, she'd know that he'd arrived where he should be.

'Hey, Emma, isn't that Freddie's phone?' Adam broke in on her musings as the phone stopped ringing and he and Lucy came clattering down the stairs, overnight bags in hand.

'Where are you two going?' Emma asked, avoiding the question while she collected her thoughts.

'Two of the centre leaders are down with a stomach bug,' Lucy explained. 'They've asked us to go back and cover their duties. And since Freddie's gone already and we get double time . . .'

'So why have you got his phone?' Adam persisted.

'It was in the marquee – he must have dropped it,' Emma replied. 'Adam, what do you know about Judy?'

He shrugged. 'Nothing,' he replied. 'Lucy did ask Freddie about her, but he just said she was history and changed the subject.'

'Funny sort of history,' Emma murmured. 'Read this.' She scrolled to Messages and shoved the phone under Adam's nose.

Adam read it, coloured and passed the phone to Lucy.

'Oh Emma,' she said, scanning the message and then

tossing the phone back to Adam and giving her a hug. 'I'm so sorry. I know how you feel about Freddie.'

'Don't worry, he's not that special,' Emma assured her. 'Now read his reply – in the Outbox.'

Two seconds later, Lucy was hugging her again. 'I can't believe he's gone rushing off to her. But you don't have to be brave,' she told her. 'We understand.'

Emma was about to come clean about her pulling ploy when the phone bleeped.

'It's a voicemail,' she said and was about to listen to the message when Adam snatched the phone back. She and Lucy watched as his expression changed from one of bewilderment, through irritation and then to sheer panic.

'Freddie hasn't turned up at the airport,' he gasped. 'His father's not a happy man. The flight is due to start boarding in half an hour. Where the hell is he?'

Lucy and Emma exchanged glances. To any female brain it was blatantly obvious where he was.

'I overheard Jake telling him not to let his father rule his life,' Emma said. 'Pity he didn't put him straight about letting some neurotic girl dominate him.' She paused, a hand clamped to her mouth. 'Hey, wait a minute!' she cried. 'We're being dim here. We've got the number for this Judy, right? Why don't we phone her and ask to speak to Freddie – that should do it.'

'Cool idea,' Lucy enthused. 'Go on then!'

'You do it, Adam,' Emma suggested. 'Just say you're the photographer ringing from Carstairs Countrywear . . .'

'On a Sunday?'

'Oh, don't be pedantic,' Emma said airily. 'These journalistic types work twenty-four seven. Just do it.'

{187}

Adam scrolled through the menu. 'Is this it, do you reckon? J?'

'Must be.' Lucy nodded. 'Go on then.'

Adam tapped his fingers, impatiently waiting for the call to be picked up.

'Hello, can I speak to Freddie Churchill please? It's really urgent. I'm ringing from . . . pardon? Well, yes, I know this is Freddie's phone – he dropped it and . . . Pardon?'

Adam's face flamed. 'Hang on, there's no need to be like that! Hello? Hello?'

He stared at Lucy and Emma. 'Some guy answered, said I was a conniving, money-grabbing bastard, told me to go to hell and rang off,' he exclaimed. '*What* is going on?'

'Emma, wait!' George came thundering down the front steps as Emma was saying goodbye to Lucy and Adam. 'I've got Freddie on the phone,' he said, waving a handset in the air. 'He's lost his mobile and he's desperate to know —'

'It's OK, I've got it,' Emma said with relief. 'Only I need to speak to him.'

'Emma's found it,' George shouted into the phone. 'What? OK then – oh, she wants to speak . . . pardon? Got you. OK, bye.'

'George, I said I wanted to speak to him.'

'Well he didn't want to speak to you,' George replied. 'He was in a rush – he'd only just got to the airport.'

'So, he's with his dad?'

'I guess,' George muttered. 'At least he paid the bill before he scuttled off. Now can I have the phone please?'

'Why?'

'Freddie wants the phone switched off and locked up in the hotel safe till he can collect it,' George explained. 'He was really stressed about it.'

'Was he now?' Lucy looked thoughtful. 'I wonder why.'

'George? You're not still mad at me, are you?'

Emma followed him into the office after Adam and Lucy had headed off in the car.

'I just can't get my head around the way you were with Lily,' he admitted, switching Freddie's phone off. 'I mean, I've always known you were controlling and wanted your own way and thought you were the centre of the universe —'

'George, I'm not like that!' A sob caught in Emma's throat.

'Lily has hero-worshipped you since she was eight,' George snapped. 'Remember how she used to hang around for hours until you deigned to let her climb into the tree house? How she helped you clean your pony's tack so that you'd reward her with ten minutes on the leading rein in the orchard?'

'I know, so that proves I'm nice.'

'Hmm. You *can* be nice,' George said, tossing the phone into the safe and turning the lock. 'You can be lovely and funny and kind – when it suits you. When it doesn't, you can be downright cruel.'

'I'll go and make it up with her,' Emma blurted out. 'Honestly, I'll tell her I didn't mean it, I'll say I'd drunk too much . . .'

'Well, that bit's true,' George agreed.

'Just say we're friends,' Emma pleaded. 'We are, aren't we?'

George looked at her unblinkingly for several seconds. Then he sighed and the corners of his mouth twitched ever so slightly. 'Friends? Yes, I guess we are.' He nodded. 'I guess we always will be.'

Relief flooded through Emma. 'I'll find Lily right now,' she said. 'I'll make it right, I promise.'

As it turned out, making friends with Lily wasn't nearly as easy as she had assumed. She ran all the way to Keeper's Cottage and banged on the door. It was answered by Jake.

'Hi, can I speak to Lily, please?' she asked, one foot already over the threshold.

'I think you've said enough to Lily!' Jake was unsmiling.

'It was a misunderstanding,' Emma began. 'If you'll just let me come in I can explain.'

'Sorry,' he said, barring her way.

'Hang on, this isn't your house,' Emma replied, struggling to keep her cool. 'You may think you can tell Freddie how to deal with his own father, but you can't tell me what to do.'

'Freddie's father? What are you on about?' Jake asked.

'I heard you, so don't pretend to me,' Emma said. 'Telling him to make a clean break, as if it was any of your business.'

She heard a cough from behind the closed kitchen door and recalled her reason for being there. 'Mrs Bates, it's me, Emma.'

There was no reply.

'She knows it's you,' Jake said calmly. 'And she told me to get rid of you.'

'Oh.' Emma swallowed hard, determined not to cry in front of him. 'I'll – I'll write a note.' She turned to go.

'Emma?' Jake called softly.

'What?'

'Just so as you know,' he said, 'I've never discussed Freddie's father with him. Anything you may have heard was about someone else.' He hesitated, his hand on the door knob. 'I really thought Freddie had explained it all to you. I'm sorry.'

Before she had the chance to ask him what he meant, the door closed in her face.

As she walked disconsolately towards Hartfield, Emma noticed the band's van parked near the lodges, its back doors swinging open. Dylan and Ravi were loading equipment and kitbags into the back.

'Hey, what's going on?' she called. 'You've got another week yet.'

'That's where you're wrong,' Dylan shouted back. 'We're heading for the big time – and it ain't here!'

As Emma walked over to the guys, desperate to find out what he was talking about, Miranda emerged from one of the lodges.

'Great news, isn't it?' she said. 'You've heard, of course?'

Reluctantly, Emma had to admit that she hadn't.

'We've only just told Tarquin,' Ravi burst out. 'See, we've got a recording contract with Mango Pippins!'

'You're joking? That's so cool!' Emma gasped, genuinely stunned by their apparent meteoric rise. 'Did my dad organise it?'

'No, it's all down to Miranda,' Dylan told her. 'See, this top guy from the label is the brother of the owner of the Mango night club chain. He read Miranda's taster piece and came to the club last week and said we were – what was it, Ravi?'

'Boundary breaking.' Ravi grinned. 'We're going to his studios to sign up.'

'Thanks to Miranda's journalistic genius,' Ravi added, throwing her a somewhat cloying smile.

'Actually, it was my father who gave you the break,' Emma said sharply.

'And me who brought them to the notice of people who matter,' Miranda added.

'I've just seen Jake,' Emma mused, ignoring Miranda's self-satisfied smirk. 'He never said a word about it.' Not, she thought miserably, that he was likely to tell her anything.

'Oh well, you know Jake. He's still pining.' Dylan laughed.

'What?' he added, glaring at Ravi who was nudging him in the ribs.

'For Caroline?' Emma said. 'I thought they split ages ago.'

'Yeah,' Dylan muttered. 'He takes things hard. Anyway, we gotta get on; this van won't pack itself.'

'Emma, wait!' Miranda caught up with her just as she reached her front door. 'Look, I can't believe this, but something tells me you're not fully in the picture,' she began.

'About what?'

'Freddie.'

'Oh, don't start that again!' snapped Emma, who just

wanted to get to her room and have a good cry.

'Emma, I'm trying to be nice to you,' Miranda persisted, 'though heaven knows why, after the way you treated poor Theo.'

'Poor Theo, as you put it, is a rampant social climber with the emotional intelligence of a disadvantaged flea,' Emma snarled. 'Actually, you seem pretty well suited.'

'Well, don't say I didn't try,' Miranda retorted. 'By the end of the week, you might be wishing you weren't quite such an egotistical little madam!'

Emma bit her lip and stalked into the house, only to bump into Harriet careering through the front door.

'I could scream! Where did Theo find that girl?' Emma exploded, gesturing to Miranda's retreating back. 'Doing charitable work in a mental institution?'

Harriet's face clouded instantly and she turned away.

'Oh God, sorry, Harriet – I didn't mean – it just came out – I'm so sorry.'

'Forget it.' Harriet kept walking and didn't look back.

And Emma burst into tears.

For the next few days, Emma felt miserable and out of sorts. Lucy and Adam, relaxed now that they knew Freddie was being the dutiful son in Rome and not lying squashed on the motorway, were busy all week taking kids from the Centre on outings to Bodiam Castle and day trips to Calais; Lily, despite the fact that Emma had sent her a really funny card and apologised more than she really thought was necessary, was still avoiding her whenever she could; and most of her other friends were jet-setting off to the Maldives or Cape Cod, and sending exotic postcards and texts that were almost too explicit in their detail about their love lives.

George's news on the Friday following the party didn't help her mood one bit. Emma found him hurling golf clubs into the back of his car when she turned up to help his mother check out the table plan for the *Midsummer Night's Dream* wedding the following day.

'Skiving off for the day?' she joked.

'No, two weeks,' he replied. 'I was just going to come and find you. I didn't want to go without saying goodbye.'

'Where are you going?' she asked, her heart sinking. 'You can't leave us in the lurch. What about the wedding?'

'Don't worry, Mum's got everything in hand – there's a whole bunch of temps coming for the day and she's interviewing new staff as we speak,' he said. 'The thing is – well, I got my MBA . . .'

'Brilliant, well done!' She gave him a hug. 'That is so cool.'

'Yeah.' He didn't sound terribly elated. 'Thing is, something's happened – something big – and I need to get away and get my head around it before I – well, before I take the plunge.'

'What is it? Can I help?'

'I wish,' he said with a sigh. 'No – this is all down to me to deal with.' He slammed the boot lid closed. 'I'm going up to Ballater. A friend of mine has a house up there and I'll do some fishing and play some golf,' he explained. 'Nothing like an eight-hour hike up Lochnagar to focus the mind.' He opened the car door, turned and gave her a quick hug. 'Be good while I'm away. If that's possible. Take care.'

And with that, he got in the car, fired the engine and drove away.

Such was the parlous state of Emma's social life that she was inordinately relieved that Harriet seemed incapable of bearing grudges. Within twenty-four hours of Emma's tactless remark, Harriet had been back to her normal self, enthusing about Annabelle Paxton-Whyte's wedding, exclaiming with delight when George's mother suggested that she could lead a party of visiting children round the Woodland Walk and Nature Trail and bursting with enthusiasm over Max's idea of a murder mystery weekend in the middle of August. So when Emma, feeling even more disconsolate after George's unexpected departure, decided that the only cure for boredom was a mega shopping trip, she invited Harriet to go with her.

'Great, super,' Harriet agreed. 'Actually, that's cool because, guess what? The doctors think Mum might be ready for a home visit next week and I need to get some stuff to brighten the place up.'

Emma was about to question whether seeing her husband's new flat might not be enough to send her mother back into the depths of despair but, remembering her past faux-pas, she merely smiled and said she was thrilled, and perhaps this was going to be a chance to put the past behind them.

'That's exactly what I intend to do,' Harriet exclaimed. 'I've made a start. Theo Elton is dead meat and to prove it, look!' She shoved her mobile phone under Emma's nose. 'Every text deleted,' she said. 'Well, there were only two . . . but I've got rid of the napkin from Mango Monkey's, and the twig he used to point out the stars . . .'

'Well done,' Emma commented, struggling not to laugh. 'And Harriet, you will find someone very soon, I'm sure of it.'

'I already have.'

'You mean – Dylan? Did I really get it right this time?'

'Dylan? Oh please. Hardly.'

'Then who?'

'Someone who rescued me when I was really at my lowest ebb . . . someone so cool, so fit, so sexy . . .'

Emma had never heard Harriet waxing so lyrical.

'I was feeling so low and scared and vulnerable and then he turned up right in front of me like that, and just reached out his hand and smiled and . . .'

Freddie. She was in love with Freddie. That was a total non-starter – Freddie Churchill, millionaire in the making, and Harriet Smith, daughter of a bankrupt? No way.

'You're sure – I mean, you're not just feeling like that because he got you out of a difficult situation,' Emma urged, desperately trying to find a gentle way to let her down. 'See, Freddie's family are really top drawer and . . .'

'Freddie? You didn't honestly think I was talking about Freddie Churchill? Oh please – credit me with a little sense! I'm not that blind.'

'But you said it was the guy who rescued you,' Emma pointed out.

'Sure. Can't you guess? George, of course.'

Emma felt as though time had stopped still, as though everything in the universe was holding its breath.

'G-George?' she stammered. 'You're in love with . . .'

She couldn't say it. This was terrible, awful, unthinkable. Harriet and George! No, no, no.

'At the party, he was just so cool, so sweet.' Harriet sighed. 'He held me so close when we danced, and he said any guy who didn't want to spend time with me must be mad and that Theo didn't deserve me.'

Emma wanted to clamp her hands over her ears to blot out the words. Her chest was tight, her mouth had gone dry and she had a sudden urge to put her hands round Harriet's throat.

'He can't, you can't . . .' Emma burst out.

Harriet's smile faded. 'What? You don't think I'm good enough for him?'

Emma didn't reply. She was grappling with the overriding emotion that blanked out all rational thought.

Harriet wasn't good enough for George. No one was good enough for George. No one, she suddenly realised with a complete shock, except her – Emma Woodhouse.

'Emma?' Harriet was peering at her anxiously. 'You don't think I'm good enough for him, do you?' she repeated, not nervously as would have been usual for Harriet, but almost defiantly.

'I didn't say that – I mean, does he . . .?' It was no good, she had to ask the question. 'Do you think he feels the same?'

No, no, of course he doesn't. She's delusional, she's crazy, Emma thought desperately.

'Actually, yes I do.' Harriet's cheeks were pink and her eyes sparkled. 'Something he said to me this morning before he went away made it quite clear.'

Emma suddenly understood why people spoke about blood running cold. The image of George standing by his car swam before her eyes: 'Thing is, something's happened – something big – and I need to get away and get my head around it before I take the plunge.'

'What did he say?' The words came out as a strangled sob.

'That's private,' Harriet simpered, and then suddenly became serious. 'You don't think – I mean, he's not the kind of guy to flirt and not mean it, is he?'

Emma bit her lip so hard that she could taste the blood. 'No,' she admitted. 'If George says something, he means it. You can be sure of that.'

'Oh great!' Harriet giggled. 'So come on, let's go shopping – I've got loads to get for Mum and with the bonus that the Knightleys gave me I can afford a bit of a splurge.'

'Actually, you go on your own,' Emma whispered. 'I think I'd better go and lie down. I'm not feeling too good.'

'I don't want Emma to hear about this, not till I've had a word.'

Emma was passing the door of her father's den on the way to her bedroom for a good howl when she heard the words that brought her to an abrupt halt.

'This is going to devastate her,' Tarquin went on as Emma held her breath, her heart thumping. 'You know how she feels about the guy.'

So it was true. Everyone knew about Harriet and George. And how come her dad realised how she felt even before she did?

She couldn't face him, not yet. But she had to talk to someone. And as usual, when she was in total meltdown, there was only one person to call.

'I got here as fast as I could,' Lucy panted, flopping down beside Emma on her bed and putting an arm round her. 'Your dad's worried about how you're taking all this.'

'So it was you on the phone?'

Lucy nodded. 'He'd just hung up when you called me. I'd been praying that he'd seen the article before you got hold of it,' she confessed. 'But, by the look on your face, you've read it already.' She squeezed Emma's hand. 'I'm so sorry, you must feel . . .'

'What article?'

Lucy pulled the latest copy of *Cheerio!* magazine from her bag.

Make your mind up, Freddie C! The headline on the centre page jumped out. Below it were two photographs. One of Freddie kissing Emma on the lips. Below it was the caption *Girl of my dreams??*

Even in her angst over George, she couldn't help taking satisfaction from the fact that she looked very sophisticated and at least twenty-one.

And then her eye caught the picture on the opposite page. It was a picture of Freddie and Jake, obviously taken somewhere in the gardens of Donwell because the fairy lights in the trees were clearly visible. It wasn't, however, the fairy lights that caught her attention. It

{199}

was the fact that Freddie had Jake's face cupped in his hands and was, quite clearly, about to kiss him.

'I don't get it,' Emma said for the third time in as many minutes. 'He can't be gay. What about Judy?'

'Not Judy, Jude,' Lucy told her. 'Like Jude Law? You must have misheard it on the phone. Jude was in the same year as Freddie and Caroline Campbell . . .'

'Caroline? Jake's ex-girlfriend? The one Lily kept going on about?'

'That's her,' Lucy confirmed. 'It's all very complicated. Apparently, Jude and Freddie were an item and Caroline was going out with Jake.'

'But if Jake's gay too . . .'

'According to Miranda, he was all confused about his sexuality and it wasn't till he met Freddie that he kind of knew for sure. Freddie broke it off with Jude and Jude got drunk and blurted it all out to Caroline, who chucked Jake.' She paused.

'So Jude was threatening to tell everyone – that's what the text message meant?'

'He'd already dropped big hints to Freddie's father,' Lucy explained. 'That's what the huge row was about – the reason Freddie came down to Sussex in the first place.'

'So if his dad already knew he was gay, what was Jude on about?'

Lucy sighed. 'Freddie had denied it,' she admitted. 'Apparently he was worried sick about not getting the shareholding due to him on his twenty-first birthday. That's why he . . .'

'. . . came on strong to me?' Emma blurted out. 'That's why he kissed me in front of Sir Douglas? And now my photograph is all over the magazine and – this is awful!'

Lucy watched her anxiously. 'It's a very good photo,' she observed weakly. 'It's the reason Miranda did it that's so horrid.'

'What do you mean?' Emma asked.

'She told Theo that she wanted to do a piece on Jake and the band, but, when they got close, she said the real reason was to make Freddie Churchill pay for what he'd done to her great mate, Jude,' Lucy went on. 'Theo contrived the invitation to the party because he knew you were mad about Freddie and . . .'

'He wanted to get his own back,' Emma concluded. 'And now I'm going to be a laughing stock with people like Serena and Chelsea. I only wanted to pull him to make them jealous. Freddie and Jake – who'd have thought it? Freddie must have sent that guitar to him – and there he was pretending not to know . . .'

Lucy burst out laughing, caught sight of Emma's thunderous expression and stopped.

'So how come you know all this anyway?' Emma demanded.

'The bit about Theo? He rang Adam and asked if we'd seen the magazine. He was really gloating.'

'And the rest of it? The bit about Freddie and Jude and everything?'

'Freddie sent this email to Adam.' Lucy handed Emma a couple of pages of A4. 'It explains everything. Including the fact that he and Jake are moving in together as soon as those share certificates are safely in the bank strongroom.'

The whole thing sounded to Emma like the plot line of a prime-time soap.

'But that's so mercenary, it's immoral,' she shouted. 'And how dare he use me like that? How dare he be so callous, so thoughtless!'

Lucy touched her hand. 'Emma, your heart must be breaking.'

'It is.' Emma could hold back the tears no longer. 'But it's not because of Freddie. I couldn't give a damn about Freddie. Jake's welcome to the two-faced, double-crossing waste of space!'

'So what on earth is it then?' Lucy gasped in alarm.

'It's George,' Emma cried. 'I love him and he's going to go off with Harriet. And if he does, I'll die, I know I will.'

So, you really think that it's just Harriet's imagination?' Emma asked Lucy half an hour later. 'Or are you saying that to cheer me up?'

'Well, I can't be certain,' Lucy began.

'So you *are* just saying it,' Emma said between sobs. 'I knew it. And yet George said she was ditsy . . .'

'Which she is,' Lucy encouraged.

'But then perhaps he's discovered he likes ditsy girls,' Emma sniffed. 'Harriet says that they talked and he said lovely things, only she won't tell me what, so it must have been dead romantic – oh, I want to throw up.'

'Emma, stop it!' Lucy pleaded. 'In two weeks, he'll be back and you can ask him yourself.'

'Ask him? I can't do that. If he says he loves her, I'll die, and if he says he doesn't he'll want to know why I'm so bothered. I do have my pride.'

'Tell me about it,' murmured Lucy. 'But just think how much worse you'd be feeling if you really had been in love with Freddie. Then you would have had something to cry about.'

So this was what love felt like. Nausea, racing heart, tears one minute, laughter the next, panic all the time. Days that dragged so slowly each one felt like a week. A face that ached from putting on a bright smile at Charity Race Day, when the few friends still in Sussex were hooked up with guys and she and Harriet were forced to be together, Harriet chatting about George and how she'd been really worried that he was shooting birds but he wasn't, it was clay-pigeon shooting, and did Emma think he'd teach her one day. And, crazy though she knew it to be, Emma had an irresistible urge to check her mobile phone for text messages every five minutes, and then spent an hour in the depths of despair when there was nothing from George.

Keeping up appearances got harder by the day. Emma's father, initially relieved that she wasn't heartbroken over Freddie's duplicity, worried when she continued to pick at her food one moment and then stuff her face with anything the fridge had to offer the next; Thalia, wracked with guilt at not having voiced her suspicions about her grandson much sooner, refused to believe that she wasn't simply putting a brave face on things, and kept coming up with diversions to keep her occupied and then worrying when Emma meekly spent a whole morning cataloguing the gallery's contents without a single complaint; and Lily, convinced that

Emma's distracted manner and constant sighing was all her fault for overreacting at the party, produced a box of her home-made fudge and a large cake with the word 'Friends?' iced on it.

At the end of the first week, she could bear it no longer. 'Have you heard from George?' Emma tried to sound casual, as she helped Mrs Knightley restock the garden kiosk with postcards and gifts before the Open Gardens afternoon.

'If I had, I'd be lying down in a darkened room to recover,' his mother said, laughing. 'Communication is not my son's strongest point.'

'Did he tell you what it was he needed to sort out?' Emma added, paying close attention to a calendar of Sussex beauty spots.

'George plays his cards very close to his chest,' Mrs Knightley told her with an amused smile. 'Something happened at Freddie's party, of that much I'm sure.' She patted Emma's shoulder. 'But I made a vow some twenty years ago that I wouldn't be an interfering mother. So, until he deigns to let me know what's going on, all I can do is wait.'

You and me both, thought Emma with a sigh.

And checked her mobile once again.

❧ CHAPTER 12 ❧

Daring dream:
Does he? Doesn't he? Will he? Won't he?

THE WEATHER FINALLY BROKE SIX DAYS LATER. EMMA, who by now was reduced to doing anything that might, just temporarily, stop her thinking about George, had been bullied by Lucy into helping out at the Frontier Adventure Centre's all-day ramble and scavenger hunt. It had seemed a good idea at the time, largely because she could take George's favourite dog, Brodie, with her and pretend George was just around the corner. In the event, it had been a disastrous decision. A violent thunderstorm when the group were at the very top of Ditchling Beacon had emptied what seemed to be a month's rainfall in half an hour, drenching her to the skin and ruining her new Kickstart trainers. In the rush to get the children back, she had left her picnic on a tree stump and was suffering from severely reduced blood sugar levels, which was probably why it wasn't until they were back at the Frontier Adventure Centre that she realised Brodie wasn't with her.

'It's an omen,' she sobbed to Lucy, after Adam had

spent half an hour calling and whistling for the dog. 'George will hate me for ever.'

'Don't be daft,' Adam said. 'Go home – I bet you the dog's got more sense than us and has run for cover. He'll turn up. Bet you.'

He was there, standing in the hall, when Emma burst through the front door of Donwell Abbey. Not Brodie. George.

'Oh!' Emma had gasped out loud before she could stop herself. In the split second it took for George to turn round, she caught sight of her reflection in the huge walnut mirror. Her wet hair was plastered to her head like a skullcap, her mascara had run down one cheek, there was a drip on the end of her nose and her cream chinos were spattered with mud.

'Emma!' George looked totally fazed to see her.

'Hi, what are you doing back? I thought you were away till the weekend. This weather is awful, isn't it? We got caught in the storm, the kids were all over the place, I've been out with Lucy and Adam, you see . . .' She knew she was gabbling but she couldn't help herself. Now that he was here, in front of her, within touching distance, she felt panic-stricken.

'It's not as bad as it was in Aberdeenshire,' said George, smiling. 'It's been raining for three days there.'

'Is that why you came home early?'

'No – no, it's not actually,' George said. 'Look – er, I was wondering – um, do you know where Harriet is?'

So this was it, she thought. All her worst fears were coming true.

'Emma?'

'I don't know – I think she's probably in the tearoom – Lily had to go to the dentist and Harriet said she'd cover for her.'

'Great. There's something I need to ask her. Don't move. I'll be back in two minutes.'

I'll have to tell him about Brodie, I'll have to stand and listen to him telling me that he and Harriet are an item and I can't bear it, I can't do it . . . Emma thought despairingly.

'Right! That's sorted.' Suddenly George was frowning, biting his lip and eyeing Emma anxiously. 'Come for a walk?' he suggested. 'I need to talk to you.'

She so wanted to refuse, to put off what she knew she had to hear, but the bottom line was that half an hour of emotional agony with George was better than a whole day without him.

'OK,' she whispered.

'Come on, dogs!' he shouted, and Emma's heart sank.

'Um, there's something you should know,' she began, as he unhooked dog leads from the hat stand. 'You see . . .'

She stopped as the dogs burst out of the games room, their paws slipping and sliding on the highly polished floor.

'Brodie!' she gasped. 'You're here.' She dropped down on to one knee and hugged the dog.

'Ah, he was with you, was he?' said George, laughing. 'Which explains why he turned up with a coating of mud and a guilty expression on his face. Did you mislay a Mars bar by any chance?' He prised the dog's mouth open and showed her distinct chocolate stains on

Brodie's teeth. Emma found herself crying with relief.

'Hey,' George said, slipping an arm round her shoulders. 'It's OK. He's a devil for running off – does it all the time. Not your fault.'

Emma gave him a watery smile.

'Come on,' George said firmly, 'Let's go.'

'Emma, will you just be quiet for five seconds!'

They had reached the copse behind Donwell before Emma had paused to draw breath. Talking about trivia was, she knew, only putting off the moment of truth. Reluctantly, she sank down on a fallen log and waited for the inevitable.

'I'm sorry.' George took her hand. 'Really I am.'

'You mean, about Harriet? It's OK,' she lied.

'Harriet? No – about lots of stuff. Freddie, for one thing. I'm not stupid – I know you fancied him . . .'

'Not really,' Emma confessed. 'I tried to – I thought it would be quite something to be going out with someone high profile. But it wasn't until Harriet . . .' She paused. There was no way she could admit to her love for him, not now. She'd just have to suffer for the rest of her life. 'You said there was something else?' Might as well get it over and done with, she thought, her throat closing with suppressed emotion.

'Oh, I'm sorry about the way I've been – bossing you about, criticising the way you carry on.'

Emma couldn't help smiling. 'Well, you've tried bossing me about since we were kids, and you've never won yet.'

George's expression was far too serious for her liking.

'And now there's something I want to insist you do,' he said, 'and I'm rather afraid that, yet again, you'll tell me where to go.'

He wants me to be happy for them, thought Emma.

'I guess, as your friend, I'll give it my best shot,' she murmured.

'I don't want you as a friend!' George raised his voice and hurled a nearby twig for the dogs. 'You don't get it, do you?'

'You mean, because of Lily . . .'

'I mean, you dim-witted ninny, that I'm fed up with being good old George, the big brother, the best friend. I love you Emma. I want us to be – a couple.'

She stared at him, blinking, half expecting this all to be a mirage, a dream that would fade in an instant.

'You mean, it's me you want? Really? But you dashed off to find Harriet.'

'So? Mum wanted help with next week's guest list and I wanted to grab Harriet, so that you didn't get roped in.'

'Oh.' Relief flooded through Emma's body like warm treacle.

'So – could you think of me as – well, not as a big brother,' George pleaded. 'I mean, we don't have to rush things if you're not sure . . .'

'Oh, I'm sure,' Emma declared. 'Very, very sure. And please, do let's rush things.'

After five minutes of finding his master locked in a motionless embrace, Brodie decided to go in search of someone else's lost picnic.

* * *

After Max Knightley and Tarquin had slapped one another on the back a dozen times as though their children's newly declared love was all of their own making, and George's mother had cried and said that Emma was just what George needed to help him loosen up a bit, Emma suddenly remembered Harriet.

'I don't understand,' George said, after Emma had confessed that her friend was in love with him. 'I never said anything that she could have misconstrued, honestly I didn't.'

'I believe you,' Emma assured him. 'She's the sort of person who gets the wrong end of the stick sometimes.'

'It takes one to know one,' George teased. 'What will you do?'

'Tell her the truth and keep my nose out of her life from now on.' Emma sighed. 'I just wish she could be as happy as me.'

'Maybe,' George remarked only half-jokingly, 'if you do just that, she will be.'

Emma sat on her suitcase, wriggling her bottom, and snapped the locks shut.

So this was it. In a few hours, they'd be on their way. She glanced round her bedroom, picked up her copy of *Australia Your Way* and stuffed it into her bag.

She was about to head off downstairs for a final briefing (otherwise known as neurotic nagging) from her over-anxious father when there was a knock on her door. She yanked it open and gasped with pleasure. Standing outside with a stunning new hair cut and the broadest grin possible was Harriet.

'Hi! Thank goodness I'm in time – I was worried you might have left already.'

'It's so good to see you,' Emma cried. Harriet had been lurking in the recesses of her mind ever since the awful day when Emma had told her that she and George were an item, and Harriet had declared that she couldn't work at Donwell a day longer, packed her bags and left. She hadn't answered Emma's text messages or emails and, when Emma, wracked with guilt, had driven over to Libby's house in the hope of news, there was a Sold board in the garden and a new family moving in.

'So where have you been? How are you? This is so cool . . . are you OK?'

'I'm just great,' Harriet assured her. 'And guess what?'

They both burst out laughing as Harriet's catchphrase escaped her lips once again.

'Go on,' Emma urged. 'Tell me.'

'Rob and me – well, we're together,' Harriet burst out.

'I know you don't like him, and I know you think —'

'Stop!' Emma said. 'I don't know him – I was so snobby and stupid and out of order to interfere in your life in the first place. I reckon I'm a bit of a control freak.'

'Really?' Harriet teased. 'I'd never have guessed.'

Emma pulled a face and gave her a hug. 'So go on, what's been going on?'

Emma listened as Harriet filled her in on how she'd taken a job in the café at the Sea Life Centre, how Rob asked her out, how his family had moved to a bigger house and were stretched for cash, so she had been renting their spare room till her dad could afford a bigger flat, and how she had never been happier in her entire life.

'You didn't answer my texts,' Emma pointed out. 'I thought you hated me.'

'At first, I couldn't face talking to you,' Harriet admitted. 'And then, we went to this cottage in Cornwall for a couple of weeks to celebrate our A-level results – oh, how did you do?'

'Two As and a B – what about you?'

'All As,' Harriet said, dropping her eyes modestly for fear of offending Emma at outstripping her. 'Anyway, we all went to Veryan – Libby and her boyfriend, and Rob and me – and there was no signal. We got back last night and I found all your texts. I'm sorry.'

'You don't have to apologise,' Emma told her. 'So what now?'

'Rob's got a place at Plymouth University to do marine biology and guess – oh, sorry! And I'm going down there to do a foundation course in music technology.' She hugged Emma. 'We're going to share a house – well, not just us, there'll be six students, but I'll see Rob every day!'

'I'm really pleased for you,' Emma said. 'And I'm sorry I messed up.'

'And I'm sorry I was so dumb about George,' Harriet replied. 'When he said he hoped I'd stop listening to you and think about the one guy who really loved me, I thought he meant him. And, of course, he meant Rob. Did you know that Rob phoned Donwell every other day to see if there was work?'

'No,' Emma admitted. 'I didn't. George didn't say.'

'Emma! Are you coming? It's getting late and Lucy's here.' Her father shouted up the stairs.

'Coming!' she called, dragging her suitcase to the door and turning to Harriet. 'I'll email you, OK? And you will keep in touch? If I promise never to interfere again?'

'It's a deal,' Harriet said laughing. 'And, er . . .' She hesitated. 'Rob's outside,' she admitted. 'Will you just come and say hi? I want you to see how lovely he really is.'

''Course I will,' Emma replied. 'But I don't need to see him to know he's right for you. You look terrific. Come on, let's go.'

Terminal Four at Heathrow Airport was heaving with people. Emma hovered by the entrance to the Departure Lounge. Now the moment had come to say her goodbyes she felt about fourteen again. There was her father, cracking silly jokes the way he always did when he was trying not to get emotional; Adam, shuffling from one foot to the other; Lucy clinging on to his arm like a limpet on the bottom of a boat. Sara and Max Knightley were hurrying back from the bookstall, Sara with a pile of magazines in her arm.

And George. Dear, darling, wonderful, gorgeous George, patiently standing there, waiting.

'Here you are, darling – something to read on the way,' Sara said, passing the magazines to Emma.

'She'll have better things to do than read,' quipped Adam.

'Adam!' Lucy nudged him and jerked her head towards Tarquin.

'Don't you wish you were coming?' Emma's question hung in the air.

'No way,' Lucy assured her. 'Two months without Adam? You've got to be joking. If you knew how much I'd been worrying about telling you I wanted out . . .'

'Now, George, you will look after her, won't you?' Tarquin insisted. 'You know what she's like – she'll get some harebrained scheme into her head and get herself into all sorts of trouble. I'm counting on you to take care of her.'

Much as Emma bristled at being talked about as if she were an irresponsible adolescent, she didn't argue. She knew she was a free-thinking, independent woman of the new millennium. But she could see no harm in being gracious enough to let George take care of her for while.

'Come on, we should go,' George urged, glancing at the departure board.

Emma hugged Lucy, Adam, the Knightleys and her

father, tears trickling down her cheek. 'I'll email,' she said. 'And phone. You too, right?'

'And George, don't you forget you're supposed to be researching eco-friendly hotels as well as bumming about the Outback, right?' Max reminded him.

'Too right,' Emma's father added. 'If I'm going to plough money into keeping Donwell open, it's going to be the greenest hotel in England – and the Aussies are good at that sort of thing.'

'I know, you told us.' George took Emma's hand firmly in his. 'We're going – now!' he ordered.

She was about to plead for one minute more but changed her mind. It was a well-known fact, as all her psychology books pointed out, that guys needed to exercise their macho tendencies in order to develop into well-rounded individuals.

And suddenly, Emma realised that for once, it might be fun *not* being the one in charge.

the Secrets of Love

Rosie Rushton

How would the Dashwood girls, in Jane Austen's *Sense and Sensibility*, fare without the restraints of nineteenth-century England?

Will Ellie's ever-sensible attitude towards life prevent her from snogging the gorgeous, but somewhat reticent, Blake?

Is Abby's devil-may-care outlook destined to land her in big trouble with Hunter, who specialises in being up himself?

And what about the baby of the family, Georgie? She's a tomboy, with more male friends than anyone, and so strong-willed she'll never take no for an answer!

'This sharp, laugh-packed take on Austen's classic story will have you grinning from ear to ear at the romantic scrapes of the three Dashwood sisters.' MIZZ

'Blends timeless truths about human nature while tackling modern teenage problems.' Bookfest

Summer of Secrets

Rosie Rushton

What would happen if the traumas of teenage life
and love from Jane Austen's *Northanger Abbey*
surfaced in the twenty-first century?

Caitlin Morland has always craved excitement.
So when she wins an art scholarship to Mulberry
Court school, she's delighted to be befriended by the
glamorous Izzy Thorpe and intriguing Summer Tilney.

As Caitlin finds herself swept up in their exotic lives,
she becomes determined to uncover the secrets
surrounding Summer. An invitation to join the
Tilneys in Italy shows her that things are very rarely
all they seem . . .

*'This is a fabulous read …Full of glamour, secrets and intrigue,
this sharp yet humorous novel will take you on a rollercoaster
ride of all manner of emotions. Rosie Rushton is one of the best
at tackling teenage problems, writing about them and providing
answers for them.'* Lovereading

www.piccadillypress.co.uk

☆ The latest news on forthcoming books

☆ Chapter previews

☆ Author biographies

☆ Fun quizzes

☆ Reader reviews

☆ Competitions and fab prizes

☆ Book features and cool downloads

☆ And much, much more . . .

Log on and check it out!

Piccadilly Press